Sala had woken up by now, too. I jumped down off my bunk and both of us stuck our heads out the train window.

"Elephants!" Sala said, throwing up her hands. She sounded exasperated.

"Elephants?" I repeated blankly.

"Look! There's a herd of them crossing the tracks." For Sala, it was a nuisance. For me, it was magical.

The moonlight was shining blue on the elephants' backs. One animal after another was crossing the track right in front of the train. They were huge and slow and graceful. Talk about amazing! Watching them was the most wonderful thing I could ever imagine. (Besides my angels, of course!)

The elephants sure took their time. They were as slow as molasses in January, as my Grandma Zoe would say. If it weren't for the time pressure I was under, I would have been happy watching them all night long.

Suddenly I heard loud screeches in the distance. They sounded almost like weird, wild laughing…

Hannah and the Angels

Searching for Lulu

by Linda Lowery Keep

Based on a concept by
Linda Lowery Keep
and Carole Newhouse

Random House New York

Cover art: © 1998 Peter Van Ryzin

 Published in the United States by Random House, Inc.,
New York, and simultaneously in Canada by Random House of
Canada Limited, Toronto.

www.randomhouse.com/kids/

Library of Congress Cataloging-in-Publication Data
Keep, Linda Lowery.
Hannah and the angels : Searching for Lulu / by Linda Lowery Keep.
SUMMARY: Continues the adventures of eleven-year-old Hannah,
who finds herself mysteriously transported to Kenya, where the
angels have sent her to accomplish a special mission.
ISBN 0-679-89080-7
[1. Angels—Fiction. 2. Space and time—Fiction. 3. Adventures and
adventurers—Fiction. 4. Kenya—Fiction. I. Title. II. Series:
Keep, Linda Lowery. Hannah and the angels; bk. #2
PZ7.K25115Se 1998 [Fic]—dc21 98-5291

Printed in the United States of America
10 9 8 7 6 5 4 3 2 1

I dedicate this book to children
from all corners of the earth.
May you each find your own special angel.

Acknowledgments

I am grateful to the people who have supported my work on this book, especially:

My husband and creative partner, Rick Cleminson Keep, who is always there with vision, encouragement, and endless patient hours of sharing ideas, adventures, and storylines;

My son Kris, and all his friends, who maximized their respect for my creative time by minimizing their volume;

All those who confirmed my research, including: the folks at the Kenyan Consulate and the Ugandan Mission to the United Nations; Gayle Bradbeer from the Denver Botanic Gardens; Micado Safaris; and Chris Baggya and Juliet Semambo Kalema for introducing me to the omululuza and its healing formula;

My sister Lori, who was my on-site field representative in Kenya;

Christine Mastro for giving me the Masai bracelet still fresh with Kenyan soil;

My terrific editor, Lisa Banim, for all her support;

Gretchen Schuler, for her wonderful design work;

And last but not least, my mother, Margaret Shanahan Lowery, who, from the time she was a girl, dreamed of seeing the animals in Kenya—and whose wildest dream came true at seventy-six.

Contents

Hannah and the Angels

Searching for Lulu

The Chess Queen

Stars, stars, stars. I just can't seem to get enough stars. Ever since I got back from Australia, I keep sticking more of them up on my ceiling—the glow-in-the-dark kind. I lie on my bed, staring up at my stars, and wonder sometimes if it wasn't all a dream.

Me, staring at the stars on my ceiling

Australia, I mean. *And* the angels. A few weeks ago, these four angels picked me up, right out of my music class, and took me to Australia. I'm serious. A boy there named Ian had asked for help tracking down some stolen endangered animals and for some reason I got picked to help him. Don't ask me why. My angels won't tell me.

I know all of this doesn't sound real. I mean, if I hadn't experienced it for myself, I'd say I dreamed it, or I made it up, or I'm totally nuts.

Except for one thing—I do have proof that I really was in Australia. I have this musical instrument called a didgeridoo right here next to my bed, and an Australian bush hat in my closet. They're souvenirs from my trip, and they're absolutely real.

It's been a few weeks now since I got back, and I keep thinking about Lorielle's message. She's the angel who sent me home with a note in my hat. In angel code, which Ian had helped me figure out with a special decoder, it said: *Next mission: Africa.*

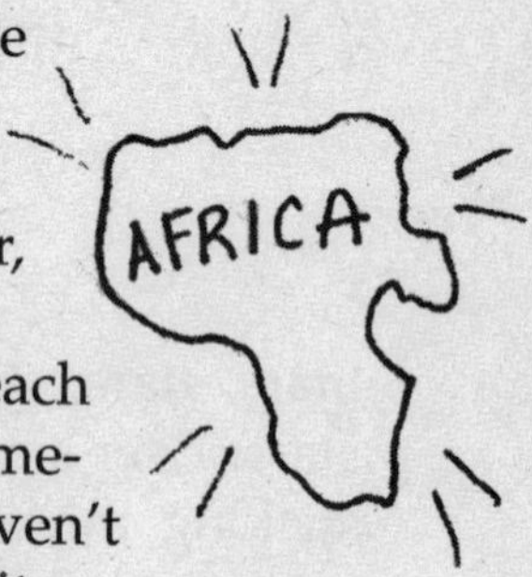

AFRICA

Oops, my phone's ringing! I reach over my dog, Frank, and my homework (which, of course, I haven't touched) and my didgeridoo to get it.

"Check," said David's voice the moment I picked up the phone. (David's my second-best friend.)

"Huh?" I said.

"I just moved my queen," he said. "You're in check."

David and I play chess together. Sometimes on the computer, and sometimes on his porch with real pieces. This game is with real pieces. We've been playing it for a while now. Both of us are pretty good chess players.

"I'll be right over," I told him.

All I had on was a T-shirt and boxer shorts, so

I quickly threw on my overalls. I didn't bother to put on shoes or socks. David and Katie, my *best* friend, live right next door. They're twins. Katie is the only person I can talk to about the angels. So far I've only told her a little bit, though. This whole angel thing is hard for even Katie to believe.

It takes exactly seventeen big steps across the grass to get to their side porch. I grabbed my backpack and was there in a second.

← 17 steps →

Running to David's house in my bare feet

"Hannah!" Katie yelled, running down the stairs when the door slammed behind me. "Did you do your social studies homework yet?"

Was she kidding? I'd been much too busy sticking up more glow-in-the-dark stars.

"Of course you didn't do your homework yet," Katie said before I could even answer. We read each other's minds sometimes. That has its good points and its bad points.

"So when you're done getting clobbered by my brother in chess, want to do our social studies together?" she asked.

"Sure," I said, ignoring the "clobbered" part. We're studying Africa in school and I have a report due tomorrow. Thinking about that, I got a little chill all of a sudden. The angel message had said my next trip would be to Africa. Maybe it was just a coincidence. Or maybe not.

I plopped down on the wicker chair across from David and looked at the chessboard. David was right, of course. I was in check. He would take my king on his next move and it would all be over.

But then I saw something David hadn't seen. My knight could capture his queen. *Yes!*

I slowly moved my knight—and dramatically pounced on his queen.

"Hello, beautiful," I said to David's queen as I swept her off the board. I dangled her in his face, just to rub it in. This was a rare occasion. To lose your queen in a chess game is the worst. She's the most powerful piece. David almost never loses his queen. Believe me, he was not happy.

"You know why the queen is so powerful, don't you?" I teased. "It's because she's a woman."

David snorted. "No, the queen's job is to take care of the king. She's just keeping him protected, so he can sit around on the couch all day, channel-surfing. It's what every man deserves."

"Very funny," I said. "The king is just a weak, useless guy."

David was completely ignoring the chess piece that I was still dangling in front of his face. For some reason, I couldn't take my eyes off her.

It was the strangest thing. She's carved out of wood, and I've looked at her a hundred times. But now, suddenly, I *really* looked at her. Her face was very beautiful, with hundreds of wrinkles. And her eyes were amazing. They seemed to be all bright, as if they were alive, staring right back at me.

David looked up. "What's wrong?" he asked, frowning.

"I don't know," I said. I was feeling a little weird. Sort of light-headed, the way I'd felt when I was playing my flute upside down and my angel Lyra swept me out of music class and transported me to Australia. In the distance, I could have sworn I heard Lyra's music, very faintly. It's ancient-sounding music, like a lullaby that makes you feel as if you're floating through centuries of stars.

I shook my head to focus on the chess game. David was quiet, contemplating his next move.

Slowly, my gaze drifted back to the queen. Her face was alive, all right. She looked positively magical. Her eyes were all sparkly like the stars on my ceiling.

She seemed to be alive

I could definitely hear Lyra's music. It was different now, with a distant drumming and soft notes from a strange kind of flute. The music got louder and louder until it completely surrounded me. I felt as if I was being captured like David's queen as the music wrapped me in its rhythmic, drumming beat.

It was happening again. The angels were taking me somewhere.

Good-bye, David. Good-bye, Katie, I said to myself.

Too bad I had left my shoes at home.

Chapter 2

A Lump on My Head

In an instant, I was sitting on the ground, wearing these sandals I'd never seen before. A bunch of kids were running around me, playing games and laughing. The queen chess piece was still in my hand.

I was playing some strange game with stones on a piece of wood. I tucked the queen in the pocket of my overalls, since I didn't need it for *this* game. It wasn't chess, that's for sure. And the boy across from me was definitely *not* David. He had dark curly hair and was wearing a red striped robe that draped from one shoulder.

The minute the boy looked up at me, he scrambled to his feet. You should have seen his face! He looked absolutely stunned. He stammered something in a foreign language. I think he was probably saying "Where did *you* come from?" or "Who are *you?*"

Before I could say "Hannah Martin," there was a thunderous crash. I ducked, shielding my head with my hands. Just in time, too. A split second later, a round green thing the size of a pumpkin fell from above and slammed to the ground beside me.

The kids leaped up and raced away. I jumped to my feet, but I was too late. *Bam!* I got slammed on the head by something hard. I collapsed, pain surging through me. I was too dizzy to get up.

The kids all came back and gathered around me. I felt them pick me up and start to carry me off. I watched everything pass by over my head, all fuzzy and pale. I saw palm trees, a huge yellow moon, a doorway, and then a whole bunch of lights shining brightly, like a grocery store.

"Where am I?" I asked weakly.

"The hospital," said a girl's voice. I was glad she spoke English.

"No, I mean...what country?"

"Doctor, doctor!" the girl yelled, sounding all worried. "She doesn't know where she is. I think she's delirious!"

She bent down toward my ear. "You are in Kenya, Africa," she whispered. "Lamu Island." She gently touched a sore spot on my forehead.

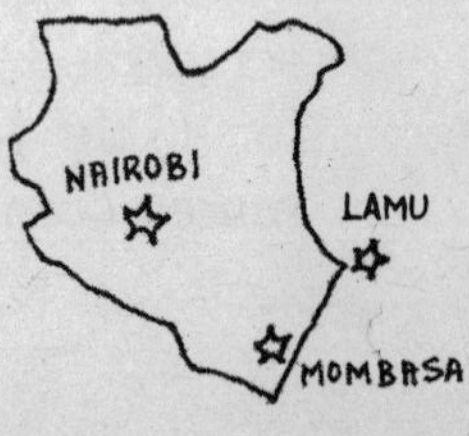

"Ouch!" I cried. "What *was* that thing that hit me?"

Maybe the girl answered, but if she did I didn't hear her. Little dark spots were starting to dance in front of my eyes. They grew bigger, then smaller, then bigger. Then there was nothing but darkness. I passed out cold.

When I woke up, I smelled hospital. You know—that clean medicine smell that makes you feel as if somebody's going to come in and give you a shot. If you've ever been in a hospital, you know what I'm talking about.

Everything around me was white. I was lying in a bed with white sheets and a white blanket and a white fan spinning on the ceiling over my head. At the foot of my bed was a white chair with my sandals and my red backpack on it.

I had a really bad headache now. I touched my forehead and felt a piece of cloth, like a bandage, covering a huge throbbing lump. What was it that had hit me, anyway? It seemed as if it had fallen right out of the sky.

I did not like this. Not one bit. I really didn't want to be stuck in some stupid hospital with a serious head lump. This was not exactly the way I'd pictured my next angel adventure.

Just then, I heard soft groans coming from the bed next to mine.

I turned my head and saw a very young girl, about six or seven, trembling under her sheet. Her face was all wet and sweaty. She looked really,

really sick. Let me tell you, it made me forget about my aching head to hear her moaning and see her little body shaking. I slowly sat up, slid off the bed, and went over to her.

"Hello," I said.

She kept on moaning. I don't think she even knew I was there. I looked at the card above her bed. It said MCHESHI. I had no idea what it meant. There was no way I could pronounce it, but I tried anyway.

"Ma-chesh-eye?" I said.

The girl's eyes flickered a tiny bit.

"Muh-CHESH-ee," said a voice behind me. "That's her name."

I spun around. It was a nurse.

"I'm Mr. Ali," he said. "I came to check that swelling on your head." He had a very nice accent. Kenyan, I guess. He led me back to my bed and started to change the bandage.

"You got hit by a large coconut," he said, dabbing something cool on my forehead.

I flinched. "That hurts," I said.

"You'll be fine," he assured me. "When it gets windy, those coconuts fly right off the trees. Very dangerous."

"I guess so," I agreed. Green coconuts? The size of a pumpkin? All of the coconuts I've seen are brown and much smaller. Well, I could think about that later.

I turned back to the sick girl. "What's wrong with poor...Muh-CHESH-ee?" I asked.

"Malaria," the nurse said, frowning. He leaned over to wipe her face with a cool cloth. "Very bad fever. Usually it is not a problem to cure these days. But I'm afraid she is allergic to the medicine we gave her. It only made her fever worse."

"How awful!" I said. "What are you going to do?"

Mcheshi moaned and rolled over, hiding her face.

Mr. Ali sighed. "We cannot find her family," he said. "Her name is very unusual, so we don't think she's from Lamu. We're not sure what to do."

"So where *is* she from?" I asked.

"We don't know," Mr. Ali said, shrugging sadly. "All we *do* know is that she needs special *dawa*."

"Special *what?*" I said.

"Medicine," he said. "*Dawa* is the Swahili word for medicine."

A chill went through my whole body. This was the reason my angels had sent me to Kenya! I just knew it! I could feel it in every cell of my body. I was here to find medicine for this sick little girl.

"Is she going to die?" I asked Mr. Ali worriedly.

He let out another long sigh. "The doctors

don't want to give her any other medicines in case she has more allergies. We are hoping her body will be strong enough to fight the fever."

Just then, someone called to Mr. Ali from out in the hall.

"But is she going to die?" I repeated.

"We hope not," he said quietly. "However, it is possible."

"Can I go now?" I asked. "I feel fine." That wasn't exactly true, but I was anxious to get started on my mission.

"You may go," Mr. Ali said. "There will be no charge for your stay. Your friends who brought you here last night made presents for the children in the hospital. We gave them to Mcheshi, to help keep her spirits up. We can take the presents as payment for taking care of you."

I spun around. The wall behind Mcheshi wasn't white. It was covered with pictures I hadn't noticed before. Pictures of green hills and colorful rainbows, spotted giraffes and huge elephants. Right in the middle of the wall was a picture of an angel. She was dressed in beautiful African clothes and a beaded necklace. She had her arms out as if she was trying to hug Mcheshi.

As I stared at the angel, I heard the distant drums again. And then a voice...

Chapter 3

Picture an Angel

"It's not her time," the voice whispered. I recognized it right away. It was Demetriel, my sort-of-guardian-angel. She had been in Australia with me, and here she was again in Africa.

"I know it's you, Demi," I said. "I'm so glad you're here."

Since nobody was around but me and Mcheshi, I figured I could talk out loud without looking nuts. Demi's voice seemed to be coming straight from the picture of that angel on the wall.

"It's not her time," I repeated slowly, trying to make sure I knew exactly what Demi had said. "Do you mean it's not time for Mcheshi to die yet?"

"Yes, Hannah," Demetriel answered. "But she's slipping away fast. She's in a lot of pain, and she's asked us angels for help."

I looked down at poor Mcheshi in the bed.

"Then *do* something, Demetriel," I begged. "Make her better."

My angel gave a long, frustrated sigh.

"You know better than that, Hannah," Demi said. "Angels can't just swoop down and fix everything. We work *with* human beings—together, like me on this side and you on earth."

Do something, Demi!

My bandage

Demi is fond of lecturing me. I am not fond of being lectured to. My mind starts to wander.

"I can help you, but I can't save Mcheshi alone," Demi continued. "It's not as if I have a bag full of magic potions up here, you know."

While she was rambling on, something dawned on me that I didn't care for one bit. I was thinking of how that coconut had tumbled down, as if it had dropped right out of the sky. Now I felt myself getting angry.

"Hannah," my guardian angel was saying, "you—"

"So, Demi," I broke in, touching my head lump. "What was the idea of chucking a coconut at me? That wasn't very angel-like, was it?"

Demi didn't answer.

"If you can chuck coconuts off trees, you can certainly save Mcheshi, can't you?"

Silence. Had Demi disappeared on me? So far,

this mission was not going very well. I guess I had to tone down my attitude if I wanted the angels' help.

"Sorry for interrupting you, Demi," I said. "But you *did* throw that coconut at me, didn't you?"

"No, Hannah, I certainly did not," Demi answered coolly.

"Then who did?" I demanded.

"Believe it or not, things sometimes happen that we angels have absolutely no control over. Aurora sent you to Lamu, but she had no idea you were going to get knocked out by a coconut. You were in the wrong place at the wrong time. You really should be more careful. I can't protect you from *everything,* you know."

"Oh," I said. At least I hadn't been conked on purpose.

"But it all worked out perfectly, though, didn't it?" Demi went on. "You found Mcheshi and got right to your mission."

"So what should I do now?" I asked.

Just so you know, Demi *never* tells me exactly what to do. She says I have to figure things out for myself, or I'll never learn anything. So I knew I wouldn't get a straight answer.

"Look, listen, pay attention," Demetriel said. "All the answers you need are right around you and inside you. The most important thing is to hurry. This child's life is going fast."

"But where do I start? I don't know anything about malaria," I wailed. "And I can't speak Swahili."

"We're counting on you, Hannah," Demi said. "We'll be here if you need us."

Then she was gone. She just disappeared to wherever it is angels disappear to.

I looked down again at little Mcheshi. This mission was way over my head. Out of my league. I'm only eleven. I have a hard enough time being responsible for my own life.

How could I possibly be responsible for saving someone else's?

Chapter 4

Who's Lulu?

I paced back and forth beside Mcheshi's bed. The angels were relying completely on me, Hannah Martin, to help this poor little girl. What if I failed? I'd probably never be sent on another mission.

But something much worse was at stake: Mcheshi might die, maybe turn into an angel herself. And like Demi had said, it wasn't her time.

I heard Mcheshi murmur something. I bent over the bed.

"Lulu," I thought I heard her say. Lulu? Who was that?

She was mumbling in Swahili, I guess.

I took my journal out of my backpack and quickly wrote down anything Mcheshi was saying that I could make out. Sometimes I've been known not to listen very well. My teacher, Ms. Crysler, always tells me that, and so does Demi. It got me in a lot of trouble on my last mission.

So this time, I listened carefully, just like Demi had told me to do. I could barely make out any words. Mcheshi kept making sounds like *ohhh* and *ahhh* and *ooo* and *loo*.

"Lulu," I heard her say again.

"Lulu?" I repeated. Mcheshi nodded and pointed for me to write it down.

"Green," she said next. She seemed to be pointing to a drawing of trees and grass by her bed.

I looked up, startled. "Did you say 'green'? Are you speaking English?"

She nodded again. I could see it was a terrible struggle for her to talk, she was so sick.

I wrote down "green."

"Leave," she said.

I figured she was telling me it was time for me to go. "Okay," I said. But first I had to try to squeeze out any more information I could. I was at a serious disadvantage here. "Is Lulu a person?" I asked gently. "Is Lulu where you live?"

She tried to say something else, but it was too much for her. She started flailing around, moaning and sweating again. I needed to get Mr. Ali.

I snapped my notebook closed. "I'll get the nurse," I said quietly. "Lulu. Green. Should I leave now and try to find Lulu Green?"

But Mcheshi couldn't answer. Her eyeballs rolled up, as if they had disappeared someplace inside her head. When Jimmy Fudge, the class clown at my school, rolls his eyes like that, everybody laughs. But this was no joke. It scared me to death.

"Mr. Ali!" I called, running toward the door.

Mcheshi looked so helpless, her tiny body all trembling. I felt as if she was the little sister I'd always wanted.

Where was Mr. Ali?

"Please, angels, please, don't let her die," I begged silently. Then I went back to Mcheshi's bed and gave her a soft kiss on the forehead.

"I'll find Lulu," I whispered. "I promise you, Mcheshi. Whatever it takes, I'll find her."

I grabbed my sandals and backpack and hurried out to find Mr. Ali. I almost ran smack into him in the doorway. I would have asked him about Lulu, but he had to take care of Mcheshi. She needed him a lot more than I did right now.

I did need help, though. I sure didn't have much to go on. How would I even begin to find Lulu? Was she a person? Was she even a *she?*

I decided my first stop would be the front desk of the hospital. They might have a map of Kenya or a phone book or something, and I could look up the names of towns. But there was no one at the front desk. Doctors and nurses hurried up and down the corridors, but no one seemed to be in charge.

I walked through an arched doorway

that led to a small courtyard. I found an out-of-the-way spot in the corner, checked very carefully to make sure there were no coconut trees over my head, and sat down.

I opened up my trusty backpack again. On my trip to Australia, the angels had magically thrown in a bunch of cool stuff I'd needed. I rummaged around inside. Sure enough, they had dropped in a few supplies. Here's what I found:

And, of course, there was my handy angel language decoder. On my last trip, another one of my angels, Lorielle, had left it with me. I had the definite feeling that another secret angel message would be showing up here in Kenya.

I unfolded the map of Kenya, but I couldn't find any town called Green or Lulu. I *did* find Lamu, though. It's a tiny island off the east coast of Kenya. It's in the Indian Ocean, which I thought sounded pretty exotic.

I got up and left the hospital. As soon as I stepped out onto the street, the sunlight made me squint. I saw palm trees everywhere and donkeys carrying people and loads of stuff like pots and blankets. Lots of women were wearing black veils that hid everything but their eyes. It seemed pretty hot to be wearing so many clothes, I thought.

And then, right in front of me, I saw the Indian Ocean! It was bright turquoise and it looked absolutely huge. Little spots of sunlight glimmered on the water like the stars on my bedroom ceiling.

I thought about the explorers in the olden days, sailing here to search for strange spices and precious jewels. That made me wonder if there are any islands that nobody has discovered yet.

If *I* were an explorer and I found a new island, I'd name it Hannah's Island and keep it all for myself. It would be completely, totally private. I'd lie in the sun and write and paint and play my flute all day long. Of course, I'd bring my dog, Frank, with me. We'd go for swims together and watch the stars come out at night. Frank would be good company. I might even bring Katie sometimes, and maybe David.

Banana Tree
PRIVATE
My own island

I stood there for a few more moments, taking in the beautiful scene. Then, as I looked up at the sky, I saw a cloud. Not a regular cloud. It was a cloud shaped like an angel. But as soon as I tried to focus on it, the cloud dissolved into thin air.

On my last trip, my angel Aurora had sent me a few messages by clouds and stars. I was sure she had sent me this angel cloud just now, but where was the message? I looked around. I didn't see any other unusual clouds, or a feather, or anything else that looked like an angel message.

I checked my watch. It's a digital watch, but now, instead of telling the time, it was flashing numbers and letters! It flashed 72 HOURS. This had to be a sign from Aurora. Then it flashed 71:59 HOURS. Yikes! What was she trying to tell me? I kept watching the numbers. They changed to 71:58 HOURS.

Oh, no! It suddenly dawned on me—71:58 HOURS must be how much time I had before Mcheshi would die! Seventy-two hours? That was only three days! Like a long weekend.

Sometimes weekends zip by too fast, and sometimes they seem to go really slowly. I spent a three-day weekend camping with my dad in northern Wisconsin once. We did a whole bunch of things. We caught fifteen walleyed pike (that's a kind of fish) and went to an Indian powwow. Then we each read a book cover-to-cover, cooked all our meals over the campfire, *and* went into town to buy a birthday present for my mom. That was a lot of stuff to cram into seventy-two hours.

I can do this, I thought. *If I use my time well, I can find Lulu and save Mcheshi in seventy-two hours.* I looked at my watch. 71:49 HOURS.

All of a sudden it looked as if time was disappearing as fast as my angel cloud!

Chapter 5

The Green Pearl

"Hey, you! Bandage girl!" I heard someone yell.

I frowned. Bandage girl? Then I remembered the gauze-covered lump on my forehead.

It was the boy I'd been playing that stone game with last night, before I got clobbered by the flying coconut. He was hurrying toward me, his game board tucked under his arm.

"So how are you doing?" he asked.

"Fine," I said, thrilled that I'd found someone else who spoke English. "Thanks for taking me to the hospital."

He nodded. "Sure. By the way," he asked, giving me a cautious look, "how did you get here last night? I'd never seen you before. Did you just fall out of the sky like a coconut?"

That made me laugh. "Is that what it looked like to you?" I asked.

He nodded again. I knew I'd better change the subject—fast.

"I thought coconuts were brown," I said. "How come that coconut that hit me was so big and green?"

"The brown part is the shell that houses the seed," he explained. "The green part is an outside rind that protects it."

I'd never thought about coconuts being seeds. I think seeds should be a more sensible size. Like grape seeds. Or cherry seeds. Much safer that way.

"Well, it was nice talking to you," I said. "I have to go now. I'm in a hurry."

"Where are you going?" the boy asked. He really did seem nice.

"I don't know," I said. It was true. I had no idea where I was going, but wherever it was, I had to get there right away.

"I have a big problem to solve," I added so I wouldn't seem rude.

"Maybe I can help," the boy said. "My name is Kisululu."

My ears immediately perked up, the way Frank's do when he hears something interesting. (Like a can of dog food being opened.) Had I heard right? Was this boy's last name Lulu?

"Keesoo Lulu?" I repeated very carefully.

"Yes," he said. "Who are you?"

"I'm Hannah Martin," I answered. "Keesoo,

do you know a girl with malaria whose name is Mcheshi?"

He shook his head. "I don't think so."

"She's looking for someone named Lulu."

The boy shrugged. "My name is not Lulu. And it's not Keesoo, either. It looks like this." He picked up a stick from the ground and wrote in the dirt: KISULULU. One word.

Well, I'd been close. His name did have "lulu" in it. Maybe that was a clue of some kind. I quickly told him about Mcheshi and how she was dying and needed help. Kisululu rubbed his chin, thinking about the problem.

"Come and play a game with us, Hannah," he said. "And we'll talk it over."

"I really don't have time for games," I said. I glanced over in the direction he was nodding and saw a bunch of kids playing. They were running around the same place I'd gotten conked on the head last night. No thanks.

On the other hand, I did have three days. And the angels hadn't steered me wrong so far. Maybe Kisululu really could help me. Maybe there was time for a *little* fun. I was pretty sure my angels wouldn't mind if I took, say, half an hour.

"Okay," I said. "But we'll have to play fast."

As we started walking, the girl who had talked to me in the hospital came up to us.

"That was a nasty accident," she said, looking at my bandaged head. "My name is Sala," she added. "I'm Kisululu's sister. I'm glad to see you're getting better."

"I'm Hannah," I said. "Were you the one who made those drawings for the kids in the hospital?"

Sala's face lit up. "You liked them? I hope they will help some children get better fast."

"Me too," I said.

Kisululu pulled out the wooden board and a bag of pebbles. I set the alarm on my watch (it was working normally again) for thirty minutes, just in case I got carried away playing. I've been known to do that sometimes.

"What do you call this game?" I asked.

"Mancala," he said.

"I've never played it before," I told him.

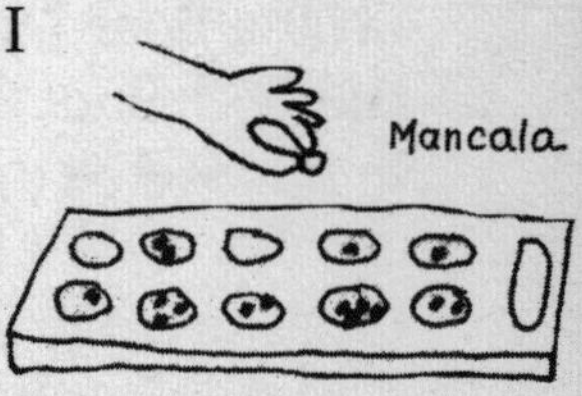

"Are you kidding?" Kisululu looked at me as if I was from Pluto or something. "Everybody plays mancala."

Mancala

"Maybe in Kenya," I said. "But not in Wisconsin. That's where I live."

Kisululu didn't ask me where that was or anything. He just said, "Okay, I'll show you." He set some pebbles into the little hollows on the board and started playing.

I caught on pretty fast. *I'll have to show this*

game to David when I get back, I thought. It's not often I get a chance to teach David something. But I was pretty sure he'd never heard of mancala.

When it was my turn, I picked up a few pebbles and held them in my hand. Just then, I heard a voice. "She is waiting for yo*uuu*..." it said.

I looked around. Nobody around me had said anything.

I went to take my turn, and I heard the words again. "She is waiting for yo*uuu*..." This time, I recognized the voice. It was Aurora's, soft and comforting. What did she mean? *Who* was waiting for me?

"Your turn," Kisululu said.

"I know," I said. I didn't want him to know I wasn't paying attention.

As I went to drop my pebbles into the hollows on the board, my hands began to feel warm and tingly. I had the strangest feeling that Aurora's hands were cupped around mine.

You won't believe what I saw then. The pebbles started growing, right before my eyes!

I *know* what you're thinking—pebbles don't grow. But I'm telling you, these pebbles kept getting bigger and bigger until they had turned into stones. They were heavy and as smooth as glass, unlike any stones I'd ever seen. They filled the whole palm of my hand.

(Did I have brain damage from the coconut?)

They were pebbles and now they were stones.

"Hello?" said Kisululu. "Are you there, Hannah?"

"Look, Kisululu!" I said excitedly. I held my hand toward him.

In the blink of an eye, the strange stones disappeared! The only thing in my hand now were pebbles—plain old mancala pebbles again.

What was going on? Had that hit on the head jumbled up my brain?

Kisululu frowned. "We have a saying here in Kenya," he said slowly. "One head cannot contain all knowledge."

"Huh?" I said.

"That means there are other people as wise as you," Kisululu continued. "Maybe if you share your problem about Mcheshi, others can help."

I nodded, still staring at the pebbles. He had a point there.

Kisululu raised one finger as if he had an idea. "Wait a minute," he said.

He called all of the other kids. When they had gathered around us, he began to tell them the whole story about me and Mcheshi in Swahili. Well, not the *whole* story—he didn't know about the angels.

Kisululu the storyteller

As Kisululu talked, he sat all straight and confident, like a wise storyteller, in his red robe. His arms were outstretched and his hands were turned toward the sky. He pointed at me a few times and made a sad face about Mcheshi. He kept repeating "lulu."

The minute he finished, a little girl spoke up.

"Do you know what *lulu* means in Swahili?" she asked me in English.

"No," I said.

"It means 'pearl.'"

"Pearl?" I repeated. Pearl! Could Mcheshi's lulu be some kind of pearl? A *green* pearl?

Just then, an alarm started beeping. For a split second, I thought it was my bedroom alarm and I had to get up and go to school. Maybe this had all been a dream. But it was my watch. Time to leave. I started to go.

"I have an idea, Hannah," Kisululu said. "Come home with me and Sala." It sounded more like a command than a suggestion. "There are healers and warriors and very wise elders in our family. You must speak with them."

"Our people are called the Masai," Sala piped in, taking my arm. (She pronounced it *Muh-SIGH.*) "Somebody there can surely help you find medicine for Mcheshi."

"Do you live near here?" I asked, feeling a little unsure. I had no idea where I should go next.

"West of here, near Nairobi," Kisululu explained, packing up the mancala game. "We are here on safari with our father."

"Safari?" I said. "Are you guys hunting animals?" That did not sound good to me.

Kisululu chuckled. "No, no. Our father came

to Lamu Island for a meeting. *Safari* means 'journey' in Swahili."

Journey? Not animal shooting? I guess I had a lot to learn about Africa.

"But I don't have much time," I reminded him. "When are you going home?"

"Today, any time now. As soon as our father finishes his meeting."

I looked at my watch. 71 HOURS. Would I have time to get to Nairobi and back?

I thought of Aurora's words: "She is waiting for yo*uuu*..."

Maybe "she" was a wise Masai woman. Maybe "she" had the medicine that would cure Mcheshi.

"She" might just have the secret of the healing green pearl.

Chapter 6

Hannah Aenda Safari

"Kisululu! Sala!" someone called.

My new friends' dad had come to get them. He was very tall and elegant. He looked a lot like my dad when he's dressed up in a suit and tie.

Kisululu and Sala ran over to their father and, in Swahili, started telling him about me.

I needed to figure a few things out before I could make a decision about visiting the Masai people, so I pulled out my journal. Things always seem clearer once they're out of my head and down on paper. Then I don't have to carry all that stuff around in my brain, you know?

My journal

I put down all of the clues I had so far. Then I checked the map for the mileage to Nairobi. I was trying to see how much time I had, considering there were seventy-one hours left.

Here's what I came up with:

CLUES

—Lulu (pearl?)

—Green

—"She is waiting for you."

—Pebbles that turn into strange stones

TIME TO SAVE MCHESHI

11 (Lamu boat + Nairobi train)

x2 (return trip—I'd have to get back!)

22 hours travel time

71 - 22 = 49 hours left

So that left me exactly forty-nine hours to search for Mcheshi's medicine.

Suddenly I realized I was being watched. I shut my notebook and saw Kisululu and Sala and their dad standing there, patiently waiting for my answer.

"I'd like to go home with you," I said. "If it's still okay."

"We'll have to ask your parents, Hannah," said the dad. "Where are they?"

Believe it or not, I had a story all worked out. And I thought it was a pretty good one.

"They're here in Kenya on vacation," I said. "I talked to them already, and they said it's fine for me to go with you, as long as I'm back in"—I glanced at my watch—"seventy-one hours."

The father looked doubtful. *Real* doubtful.

"They already gave me money for the ferryboat and the train." I showed him my Kenyan shillings.

"I would rather meet your parents first," he said, hesitating. "But we would have to leave now to catch that train on time."

He checked his watch, and I checked mine. No flashing numbers, thank goodness.

"All right," the father finally decided. "We can call them when we get to Nairobi, so they'll know you've arrived safe and sound."

"Great!" I said. I figured I'd cross *that* bridge when I came to it. At least I'd have some time to think up a plan by then.

Kisululu and Sala ran to get their suitcases from under a tree. Their dad was carrying his. I slipped my pack on my back.

"So," said the dad, smiling. "Hannah aenda safari."

"What does that mean?" I shot a questioning look at Kisululu.

"It's Swahili. It means, 'Hannah goes on a journey,'" he said. It sounded like the title of a story to me. Ms. Crysler (everyone in my class calls her Ms. Crybaby) would eat this one up. Automatic "A."

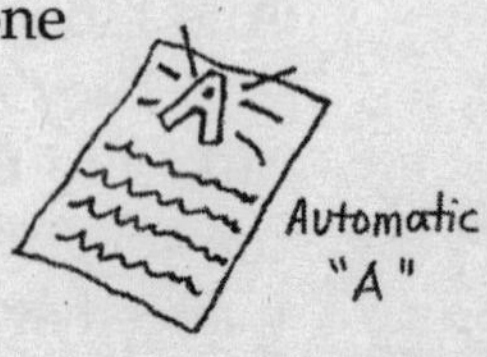

We walked across town to the boat dock. While we waited for the ferry, I wrote a short story. (Very short.)

"Hannah Aenda Safari"
by Hannah Martin

Hannah is in Africa. She must save a girl who is dying of malaria. A fearless adventurer, she journeys to find a wise Masai woman who knows about Lulu, a magical green pearl. The wise woman cures the dying girl using Lulu's ancient healing magic. Hannah is sent home. Her safari was a great success.

THE END

Wouldn't it be perfect if that was the true story of what was going to happen? Maybe 70:45 hours from now, there'd be one big, happy ending. Mcheshi would be magically cured, and we'd be pen pals forever.

That's what's great about writing stories. You can make them turn out any way you want. Of course, my journal story was nothing like what happened in real life. Not even close.

My safari started out great. I was thrilled to cross the Indian Ocean, even a tiny part of it. The problem was, after the Indian Ocean, the whole safari started to go downhill.

What happened first was that Kisululu and Sala's father pulled out his train ticket on the boat. I noticed it said "Mombasa-Nairobi," not "Lamu-Nairobi." I checked my map. Mombasa was a city, and it was *way* out of the way!

"Why does your ticket say the train leaves

from Mombasa?" I asked him, confused.

"Because it *does* leave from Mombasa," he answered.

"But Mombasa isn't even on the way to Nairobi!" I objected. I checked my map again. Maybe I'd made a mistake.

"There are no good roads between Lamu Island and Nairobi," he said. "And there are no direct trains."

"So we take a bus south to Mombasa," Sala explained.

"Then we take the train northwest to Nairobi," Kisululu added.

This was terrible! "How long will this safari take?" I asked. I didn't have one single minute to waste.

"Oh, we should be in Nairobi in about eighteen hours," Kisululu said.

"EIGHTEEN!" I cried. "We'll be *sleeping* on the train?"

This was more than terrible! The whole situation was becoming a nightmare!

"And then we take a plane from Nairobi to our family," Sala finished.

"Plane?" I cried. This was *not* good. A boat, a bus, a train, then a *plane?* What was I doing? This was completely insane!

"I thought you guys lived in Nairobi!" I wailed.

"We *do* live in Nairobi," explained the dad

very softly. "That is where I work." I think he was trying to calm me down with his "library" voice. I probably sounded hysterical. I was.

"But our real family are the Masai people," he went on. "They live out on the plains. Sala and Kisululu are going there to visit their grandmother. You are going with them."

Now I thought I was going to totally lose it. I wanted to stomp my feet and throw a fit like a two-year-old. What a waste of precious time!

"Then I have to go back to Lamu," I said firmly. "Right now!"

By this time, we were already off the ferry and on the Mombasa bus. I hoisted my pack on my shoulders. I'd have to get off at the next stop and head straight back to Lamu.

Sala touched my shoulder. "We don't often invite strangers home," she said gently. "I think it is important for you to come with us."

"Thank you very much for inviting me," I said. I didn't want to be rude. "But I'm on a mission. Mcheshi has less than three days to live. I can't possibly spend a whole day getting to your family and a whole day getting back!"

Just then, I saw something out the window. My angel cloud! It was back, flying alongside the bus! I took a deep breath and sat back down in my seat.

I was about to get another message from Aurora!

Chapter 7

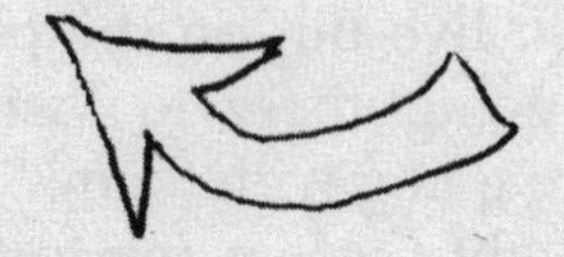

Trains, Planes, and Elephants

"Look at that cloud," said Sala, peering out the bus window. "It looks like an arrow."

It sure did. I had been watching the cloud change shape from an angel into an arrow.

"It's pointing south, isn't it, Sala?" I said.

"Yes," she answered, nodding. "South toward Mombasa."

My angel cloud

It looked as if I was going the right way after all. The message was very clear, at least as far as angel messages go. They can be confusing sometimes. I would just have to trust that Aurora would not let too much time run out.

So Mombasa it was! The road was long and bumpy. It took *forever*.

I asked Sala a zillion questions on the way. I wanted to get all the information I could.

"Have you ever heard of a green lulu pearl?" I asked her.

She raised her eyebrows. "I've never heard of green pearls," she said.

Too bad. I figured if anyone knew about green pearls, it would be Sala. I think she knew a lot about jewelry. Oh, I forgot to tell you what Sala was wearing. How could I forget? Her jewelry was so cool. She had bracelets on her wrists and ankles, a headband, and a really beautiful necklace. They were all made of beads of every color. Katie would drool for jewelry like Sala's. I don't wear very much of it myself. Usually just my watch.

"Do you ever wear pearls?" I asked Sala.

"No," she answered. "Only beads."

I felt majorly dull sitting next to Sala. I sure could use a little sprucing up. I eyed her necklace. I really wanted to try it on, but I felt a little funny asking her. It wasn't like I had anything interesting of my own for her to try on. I hadn't exactly had time to plan my wardrobe for this trip, you know?

"Would you mind, Sala," I asked bravely, "if I tried on your necklace?"

She smiled. "Not at all. I made it myself." She took it off and handed it to me.

Sala's necklace was made of rows and rows of

beads strung on something stiff, like wire. She fastened it carefully around my neck. I checked out my reflection in the bus window. It didn't exactly go with my overalls, but who cared? I looked exotic. Like a *National Geographic* cover girl or an African queen. Sala let me wear the necklace all the way to Mombasa.

I told you I sometimes get distracted. I suddenly realized I had to forget about wardrobe experiments and focus on my mission. I stared out the bus window, trying hard to concentrate. The view was awesome. I saw a herd of giraffes running in the tall grasses—moms, dads, kids, and babies, all galloping along. I also spotted a couple of warthogs, which I loved. I wonder who came up with that name? It sounds like a hog with some kind of wart problem.

Anyway, after the boat and the bus, the four of us got on a train. I had never been overnight on a train before. The rooms had tiny sinks and these little bunk beds. Sala and I shared a room. I took the top bunk. Sala took the bottom.

I changed my bandage, which was pretty gross and ratty by then, and put on a clean one they'd given me in the hospital. Then I tucked my journal under my pillow and got into bed. The train was making this peaceful rhythmic sound. It had a sleepy, steady beat, kind of like those drums I'd heard with Lyra's music. It put me right to sleep.

In the middle of the night, a low rumbling noise woke me up. Then the noise stopped. Something was wrong. But what? It took me a minute to figure it out. Then I realized our train had stopped! It must have broken down!

I looked at my watch. It was flashing angel time again. It told me: 57 HOURS.

Sala had woken up by now, too. I jumped down off my bunk, and both of us stuck our heads out the train window.

"Elephants!" Sala said, sounding exasperated. She threw up her hands.

"Elephants?" I repeated blankly.

"Look! There's a herd of them crossing the tracks." For Sala, it was a nuisance. For me, it was magical.

The moonlight was shining blue on the elephants' backs. One animal after another was crossing the track right in front of the train. They were huge and slow and graceful. Talk about amazing! Watching them was the most wonderful thing I could ever imagine. (Besides my angels, of course!)

The elephants sure took their time. They were as slow as molasses in January, as my Grandma Zoe would say. If it weren't for the time pressure I was under, I would have been happy watching them all night long.

Suddenly I heard loud screeches in the distance. They sounded almost like weird, wild laughing.

"What is *that?*" I asked Sala nervously.

"Hyenas," she said. "They're after the young elephants."

The hyenas were definitely not laughing. The elephants all gathered together and formed a circle, like kids playing ring-around-the-rosey.

"What are they doing?" I asked. Sala was probably an elephant expert. After all, she'd lived around them all her life, the way I live around squirrels. The only elephants I'd ever seen were either on TV or in the zoo.

"The babies and young elephants are inside the circle," she explained. "The adult elephants are protecting them from the hyenas."

Now I thought *that* was the most wonderful thing I could ever imagine. (Besides my angels, again.) It made me think of Mcheshi. She needed all the protection she could get right now. I wanted to be one of those big elephants, keeping her safe.

Circle of Elephants
(babies inside)

The elephant herd blocked our train's path—and the hyenas'—for about an hour, then lumbered away into the darkness. The train headed northwest again.

We finally, *finally* got to Nairobi, which was a huge, busy city, and grabbed a taxi to the airport. Kisululu and Sala's father would not take money for the plane ride. He said the pilot was a family friend and was going out there anyhow. That was a lucky break. I wasn't sure if the angels had left me enough money for a plane ticket.

By now, I was dragging along like a rag doll. My feet hurt, the lump on my head hurt, and my hair was hanging all droopy. I felt as pale as a sick cow.

Kisululu, Sala, and I got settled into this cool little plane. The pilot had blankets and snacks for us.

"You're all set," said Sala and Kisululu's dad. "I just need your parents' phone number, Hannah, and then the pilot can take off."

Rats! I'd forgotten to think up a plan!

"I don't know the number of their hotel by heart," I said. "It's buried somewhere in my backpack. I'm not sure I can dig it out right now."

"Just tell me the name of their hotel, then," he said. "I'll find them."

Yikes! This dad was too quick! I'd have to try another tactic.

Kisululu came to my rescue. "Hannah will be okay," he told his dad. "We'll make sure she calls."

His father gave me an exasperated look. But what could he do?

He kissed Sala and Kisululu good-bye and shook my hand.

When the plane took off, I closed my eyes. When I opened them again, it was morning. We were there!

A tingling feeling rushed through me. For the first time, as we gathered our bags and prepared to head toward the bustling Masai village, I felt as if I was in the absolute right place to find what I needed for my mission.

Chapter 8

Too Many Questions

Sala's first words off the plane did not make me happy.

"Come with us to school," she said.

Was that the worst idea in the world or what?

"No way!" I said firmly. "I have way too much to do."

"I think school is the perfect place to start," she said. "Our teacher and our friends might have some ideas for you."

I looked at Kisululu. He just nodded.

Sala took my hand and led me through a group of busy women. They were all dressed like Sala, with shaved heads, red clothes, and lots of beaded necklaces and other jewelry. They were standing over huge pieces of animal skins spread out on the ground everywhere.

"What are they doing?" I asked Sala.

"Drying cowhides in the sun," she said. "And if you don't come to school, you'll have to work on the cowhides with them."

So guess where I went? Kisululu joined us after he'd run to his grandmother's house to tell her that we had arrived safely. He brought me a handful of stones.

I checked them out right away. I thought maybe they were special stones like the ones that had showed up when I was playing mancala. These didn't grow or anything. They were just regular stones.

As we walked to the school, Sala and Kisululu tossed their stones into the tall grass ahead of us.

"What are you doing that for?" I asked.

"To keep the lions away," Kisululu said.

"And the black mamba snakes," Sala added.

I laughed. They had to be kidding.

"We're serious," Sala said. "You always want to warn the animals that you're coming so they can clear out of the way."

Yikes! I quickly started tossing *my* stones into the grass, too. Things sure were different here!

School was different, too. First of all, the classroom—the only one—was outside, blackboard and all. We sat on the ground. And the teacher was amazing.

He was dressed in a flowing red and blue cape, and he carried a walking stick. He looked proud and calm like a king.

Immediately, the kids stood up and said,

"Jambo, Mzee." I figured out pretty quickly that *jambo* means "hello". (I found out later that *mzee* means "sir" or "elder".)

Wow! This was nothing like Kennedy Middle School when Ms. Crybaby comes into class. She has to yell to get us to take our seats, and there's always some clueless kid who's lost by the lockers or stuck in a bathroom stall, and Ms. Crybaby has to send some student off to find them. (The clueless kid is usually Jimmy Fudge.)

Class started, and the teacher asked everyone to speak English because Sala and Kisululu had a guest from the United States. (Guess who?)

The teacher suggested that I introduce myself to the class.

"Okay," I said, getting to my feet. This would be a perfect chance to see if anyone could help me with my search! The minute I got to the front of the class, everybody raised their hands with questions. Most of the questions were about snow.

"What does snow sound like? Is it loud, like rain?"

"What does it taste like? Like coconut milk?"

"When it snows, do the animals get covered and die?"

I had never even thought about stuff like that

before. I have to admit, I kind of rushed through their questions so I could get on with my own. I finally got a chance to tell them about Mcheshi, and the green pearl, and how I was in a major hurry and had to be back in less than two days.

As soon as I finished, a girl raised her hand.

"My name is Lulu," she said.

Could she be *the* Lulu? The one who Aurora said was waiting for me? I rushed over to her.

"Do you know how to heal malaria?" I asked.

The other kids snickered, but Lulu didn't.

"No," she said. "But my aunt is a doctor. She teaches me a little about healing sometimes."

The teacher quickly broke in to say that kids don't heal people. Elders do. I guess it's like somebody asking me to heal their sick pig just because my dad's a veterinarian. I'd laugh, too.

"But do you know anyone named Mcheshi?" I asked Lulu. I wanted so badly for her to be *the* Lulu.

"No," she said. My heart sank. Obviously, she wasn't the one I was searching for.

Some other kids raised their hands. They were all worried about Mcheshi and were full of ideas. I opened my journal to take notes.

"Tanzania has many diamond mines," one girl said. "Maybe they have magical green pearls there, too."

I wrote down "Tanzania."

"Uganda is called the Pearl of Africa," one boy told me.

"Really?" I said. Now I was getting confused. Could Uganda have something to do with my search? I wrote down "Uganda."

"My grandma is an herbal doctor," Kisululu spoke up. "But she's very old and sick now." I made a note of that, too.

"Maybe the *laibon* knows about a green lulu or a special pearl," said the teacher.

"LY-bon?" I asked, scribbling away again.

"The medicine man," the teacher answered. "He might not see you, but you could try."

That idea sounded really good to me. I wrote down "medicine man."

"Any other ideas for Hannah?" the teacher asked the class.

I was relieved that nobody else raised their hands. I had too many ideas already. They were beginning to boggle my brain.

Tanzania? Uganda? Herbal doctor? Medicine man?

My head was spinning. I looked at my watch: 44:15 hours left! I had too many questions—and not one single answer.

Chapter 9

Firelight Drums

After school, I learned about the cow dung. Yuck. Not that *that* had anything to do with Lulu.

"Here is my aunt's house," Sala said as she showed me around the village (which she called the *enkang*). "My grandmother is ill, so we'll stay here." The house was small and roundish, the color of baked clay. It had one opening for a doorway and no windows.

"The women build the houses," Sala explained. "They make them out of cow dung."

I thought I heard wrong. "Cow dung as in... *cow pies?"* I asked.

"Yes," said Sala. "We shape the houses with long sticks and then lay wet cow dung over the sticks. It makes very sturdy homes."

Well, I guess you

House made of cow dung
(It doesn't smell bad at all!)

have to use whatever's handy. The Masai had plenty of cow dung from all their cattle, I'll tell you that much. I was dodging cow pies all over the place.

I dared myself to scrunch my nose up against the wall. I sniffed. It smelled just fine, like regular dry dirt or clay. Not what I'd expected, thank goodness.

"You look tired, Hannah," Sala said. "Why don't you go in and rest up?"

Sala must have read my mind. Our safari had worn me out, and I had a busy night coming up. When the family got together later, Sala and Kisululu were going to help me tell them about my problem.

Inside, the dung house was actually cozy. There was one room with a fire burning in the middle. On the sides were two tiny rooms. They were built up high, with cowhide quilts you could sleep on.

I crawled onto a bed, curled up, and fell fast asleep.

I dreamed about Aurora. She was flying through the night sky, and I was flying right behind her. She had a basket of stars in her arms. She was throwing the stars out to make a path for me.

She was telling me in her reassuring voice: *The answer is right here. You have all the time you need. Be here and know that she is waiting for you.*

I woke up and wrote down the dream in my journal right away. I read somewhere once that that's what you're supposed to do with dreams. Otherwise you'll forget them and you'll never be able to figure out what they mean.

My Star Path Dream

That's when the next strange thing showed up. I turned to the page where I'd drawn the picture of the green pearl. I swear when I looked at it, I saw a face in the pearl. It was an old man with deep, mysterious eyes. I had no idea who he was, but I saw him clear as day.

"Is this guy here in the village?" I asked Aurora. But I didn't get an answer. When I looked down at the page again, his face was gone.

I closed my journal, feeling a little disappointed, but much calmer. Aurora had told me to stay right here in the village and watch for signs. That meant no rushing off to Tanzania or Uganda. The answers had to be right here, under my nose.

When I stepped outside the hut again a little while later, everybody seemed to ignore me, as if I was just part of the scenery. I was kind of glad about that. That way, I could quietly watch for more angel signs and messages without feeling as if I stuck out like a sore thumb.

These Masai people seemed to have their routines down pat. First the women made dinner. Sala and I were in charge of making *ugali,* which is cornmeal mixed with water. (Easy!) Luckily, I wasn't in charge of the milk. The Masai women were mixing it with cattle blood, straight out of the neck of the cow. It's good for you, they told me. That was one thing I didn't have the guts to try!

I decided to keep an eye out for a woman who looked as if she might be waiting for me. So far, I hadn't seen anybody.

Soon all of the men came back from grazing the cattle. They were dressed in red clothes, with necklaces and earrings and headbands. They looked as if they were going to a party instead of coming home after having worked in the fields all day.

As they came by, I checked each of their faces, trying to see if one was the old man I'd seen in my green pearl picture. Nope.

The next part of the Masai routine was to keep the lions out of the village for the night. Kisululu helped the men cover the entrance to the village with big branches, which had enormous thorns on them, the size of knives. So now we were all safe and sound. (I hoped.)

After the sun set, all the kids sat around the fire and one of the grandfathers told stories. I looked closely at his face. He wasn't the one from the green pearl picture, either.

Sala translated for me. "He's speaking Maa," she said.

"Maa?" I asked. "I thought you guys spoke Swahili."

"There are a thousand languages in Africa," Sala told me.

A thousand! I couldn't believe it! How could anyone understand anyone else?

"We speak Maa here at home. In Nairobi we speak Swahili. With my grandmother, I speak Lugandan."

"And with me, you speak English," I added. Wow! I was impressed.

During the storytelling, something suddenly dawned on me. How did I know that Mcheshi had been speaking Swahili? I knew she'd said "green" in English. But maybe *lulu* was a word in one of those thousand other African languages. *Uh-oh.*

"It's your turn," Kisululu said just then.

"Huh?" I asked. "What do you mean, my turn?"

"They want you to tell them about Mcheshi. But first they'd like you to sing a song or tell a story."

"But I can't sing!" I said, panicking. "And I don't have any good stories."

"You can do whatever you want," said Kisululu. "I'll translate."

"Thanks," I said with a sigh.

I ended up telling a really stupid joke about lions. I'm sure you've heard it:

There's this guy hopping down the street on one foot, tooting a horn. His neighbor sees him and thinks he's crazy.

"Why are you hopping down the street on one foot, tooting a horn?" asks the neighbor.

"It keeps the lions away," says the man.

"But there aren't any lions around here," the neighbor says.

"See?" says the man, all proud of himself. "It's working."

My joke

Kisululu just sat there without moving when I finished, like there was supposed to be more.

"Is that the whole joke?" he asked.

"Yes," I said.

"Okay," he said, frowning a little.

He translated my joke. Everybody just sat there. Nobody laughed. I was really, really sorry I'd tried to tell a joke. I guess it's hard to make people laugh in a different language.

"Let's tell them about my mission," I quickly told Kisululu. Maybe they'd think that was more interesting. Kisululu sat in his confident storyteller pose, the way he'd sat with the kids on Lamu. When he had finished explaining, he talked to the people a little longer. Then he turned to me.

"Nobody has any answers for you yet," he said. "But everyone will help."

"But can't anybody help me *now?*" I pleaded. I had less than thirty-six hours left.

"They will," he said. "They will."

A drumbeat interrupted our conversation. The evening was ending with music. Everybody began to pull out drums and flutes and instruments with strings that I'd never seen before.

"Do you think they'd mind if I tried to play with them?" I whispered to Sala.

"Of course not," she said.

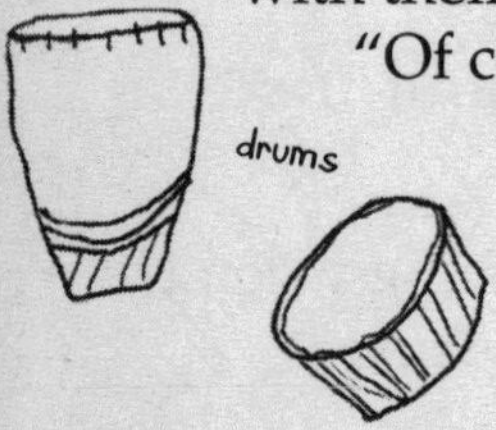

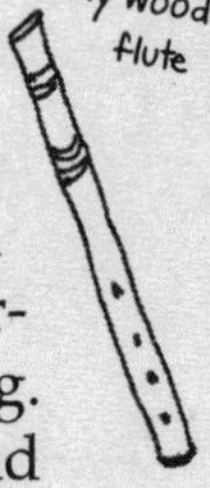

Out of my backpack, I pulled the wooden flute that the angels had left me and joined in. The music we made was so mysterious, with the drums and flutes mixed in with Lyra's music. For a few minutes, I forgot about time and just played along. The drumming grew louder and louder. Then some people started dancing. I watched the firelight cast shadows on their red hair and their colorful beads.

Suddenly, without warning, everything stopped. There was an eerie silence. Everyone was gazing past the fire at someone walking into the group.

I looked, too. The newcomer was a very old

man in long red robes, walking with a stick. Instead of feathers or beads, he wore a knit cap like a hockey cap on his head.

As he got closer, the firelight danced in his dark eyes. I recognized him right away.

He was the man from the green pearl!

Chapter 10

Bones and Stones

For a split second, I felt totally paralyzed. How could it be that I had seen this man's face in my journal picture and now here he was in real life? It seemed impossible.

The old man moved through the crowd, straight toward me. Everybody had grown dead silent. All I heard was the crackling of the fire.

He stopped and sat down just a few feet from me. Slowly, he opened a small bag and pulled out some things that looked like bones. Then he shook a few stones out of another bag.

I looked at the stones and gasped out loud! They were just like the ones I'd seen when I was playing mancala! The same strange, smooth stones! (Later Sala told me those stones are very old and come from the stomach of a giraffe.)

I knew for sure that this man had to be the

laibon. I never imagined I'd meet a medicine man for real—and here was one right in front of me! I was sort of creeped out, but I was excited, too.

The *laibon* gazed at me for a long time. I squirmed a little, feeling uncomfortable. What was he staring at?

"I was called here," the medicine man said finally in Maa. (Sala translated for me.) "I do not know why."

Had my angels sent him here? I wondered.

He asked me a few questions about Mcheshi and the green *lulu* medicine. Then he silently rolled the stones around in his hand.

The laibon

"The child will live," he said.

"But without *dawa* Mcheshi will *die!*" I insisted. I might as well get straight to the point. "Do you have a magic green pearl that will cure her?" I asked him.

The medicine man shook his head and rolled the stones carefully in his fingertips. It was so mysterious, as if he was reading the stones with his fingers.

"I am not a magician. I am a doctor. I have no green pearl," he said.

I guess he set *me* straight. But since I'd never met a medicine man before, I didn't really know if he was a doctor or a fortune-teller or what.

"Besides," the *laibon* said, looking into my eyes, "it is not a pearl that you seek."

"No?" I have to admit I was very disappointed to hear that. I loved the idea of a healing green pearl. It seemed so romantic and magical. Maybe he was wrong.

"Then what *am* I looking for?" I asked.

The medicine man closed his eyes. I got the feeling he was listening to his own angels, and I wondered what they looked like. Probably very colorful, with wings like tropical birds.

"It is a woman you must find," he said finally.

Yes! Now we were getting somewhere!

"A woman who speaks the child's language. A woman who comes from the child's native land," the medicine man continued, his eyes still closed. "She also heals, but with neither stones nor pearls."

"Who is she?" I asked. "Is she named Lulu? Where is she?" I wanted to find her right away.

"She is here," he said.

I immediately remembered Aurora's words in my dream: *Be here*. This mystery woman had to be somewhere here in the Masai village.

"She knows you are coming. She is waiting for you."

Now I got major chills. Those had been Aurora's words exactly: *She is waiting for you.*

"So how can I find her?" I asked impatiently.

"I can see that you are being guided," the *laibon*

said. "Stay on your path, and soon you will find your medicine."

"*What* path...?" I began, but Sala held up a finger to silence me.

"Shhh!" she whispered. "He's finished."

The *laibon* rose to his feet. He was finished, all right. He passed by the fire, moved through the silent crowd, and left. I have no idea where he went. He simply disappeared.

I just sat there, stunned.

I have to tell you, I was bummed. I guess I'd wanted the medicine man to solve my problem for me—to give me the answer straight out. I'm like that with my angels, too. It would be nice if I didn't have to do so much of the work myself. It's not that I mind, of course. It would just make things so much *easier*.

I walked back to the hut with Sala and climbed onto the bed. I felt as if I was floating in a dream. *What happens next?* I wondered. *What should I do to find this mystery woman who is waiting for me? Why doesn't she come and find* ME?

When I closed my eyes, I kept searching for a face. Would this woman show up the way the *laibon* had? Would I see her in a dream?

But much too soon, dawn came and I was awake. I hadn't seen a face. I hadn't gotten a message. I still had no idea who *she* was. I looked at my watch. Thirty-nine hours and counting.

Chapter 11

Back to Square One

I grabbed some breakfast and left the *enkang* early to go for a walk. I was desolate. That's a David word: *desolate*. If I can't find the exact right shade of lavender hat or pink tights, he says that I overreact and seem *desolate*. Right at this moment, hats and tights seemed pretty frivolous. This was a life-and-death situation. I was really, truly desolate.

I had thirty-nine hours left, barely enough time to get back to Lamu. How could I possibly have time to find this mystery woman and get *dawa* for Mcheshi? I knew Sala and Kisululu and everyone in the village would try to help me. But we sure didn't have much time.

I sat down in the tall grass and took out my journal. What clues did

Me and my journal in the grass

I have so far? I crossed out "Uganda," "Tanzania," and "healing green pearl." I added the clue from Aurora and the *laibon* about a woman, somewhere, who was waiting for me.

Here's what I had now:

1. Mcheshi's words: Lulu, green, leave
2. Sala and Kisululu's grandmother (an herbal doctor)
3. Mystery woman nearby who speaks Mcheshi's language (whatever it is!)

Wait a second! Maybe I had something here! Couldn't Sala's grandmother be the mystery woman? Of course she could! She was an herbal doctor! And she lived in the village! Why hadn't I gone to her right away?

I jumped up and started pacing in circles, thinking. I do that a lot.

But wait! Sala's grandmother wasn't from another country. She didn't speak another language. If she lived here in the village, and she was Sala's grandmother, then she had to be Masai. That blew my whole new theory. *Rats!*

I stopped pacing and sat back down, feeling desolate again. My skin was all crawly and sweaty, the way it gets when I panic. I was getting absolutely nowhere.

And in my mind every time I closed my eyes, I saw Mcheshi's little face. I knew she was growing sicker and weaker by the hour. Her eyes were pleading for me to save her.

"Angels!" I called out loud. "Help me! I need some kind of sign. A message. Anything. I need to know what to do next."

I waited a little while to give my angels a few minutes to show up. I doodled some little squiggles in my journal. Well, maybe my angels needed more than a few minutes to fly in from wherever they were. So I waited a little while more and drew a few more squiggles.

"Don't all rush to my rescue at once!" I finally yelled sarcastically.

There was no answer. No music, no message, no angel cloud.

I looked down at my squiggles. They reminded me of that chess piece from my game with David. I still had the queen in my pocket. I pulled her out and held her in my hand. Maybe I could sketch a picture of her to keep me busy while I waited for my angels to get back to me.

As soon as I started drawing, I heard familiar music in the far distance. It was Lyra's music, for sure. I kept on drawing, and the music got louder. To experiment, I stopped drawing. The music got quieter. This was amazing!

Now I drew faster and faster. I sketched the queen's hair, then her face. The minute I finished,

I was completely surrounded by the music. I knew what *that* meant. I was being transported! Lyra was sending me someplace, but I had no idea where.

Suddenly I was back home, sitting across from David again. We were right where we had left off in our chess game. Not one single second had passed! He moved his bishop.

"Checkmate," he said, all smug.

I didn't even care that David had won the game. I was clutching the queen exactly the way I had been when I left for Kenya, and I knew—I just *knew*—that Lyra was trying to tell me something important.

Could it be that I had the answer right there in my hand?

Chapter 12

Telling Katie

"Hey, Hannah, what's that on your head?" David asked, leaning forward and peering at me strangely.

I suddenly remembered the coconut lump. I could not think of a single half-intelligent thing to say. How could I have gotten hurt sitting right here at the chessboard, on David's porch?

"Ummm…I hit myself on a door when I was running here?" I said sheepishly. David was still staring at me, as if he was worried there might be something terribly, pathetically wrong with me.

I felt a little strange. Fuzzy. I wasn't quite back from Kenya yet. I needed to talk to someone. Not David—at least not yet.

"Katie?" I called. She was practicing her cello in the front room.

"Are you all right, Hannah?" Katie asked,

stepping out onto the porch. When she saw me, her eyebrows had raised way up under her bangs.

"I'm fine," I said shakily. "But I need your help right this very second." I tucked the queen chess piece back in my pocket and grabbed my backpack. Then I followed Katie upstairs to her room. We usually do our homework up there. David started after us, open-mouthed, but he stopped on the landing. He knew better than to follow us. I felt kind of sorry for him, but I couldn't explain everything right now. I didn't have time. I'd make it up to him later.

Squirt, David's ferret, followed us up the stairs. I can't say I'm terribly fond of Squirt. He smells like an old basement most of the time. But he's just right for David—cute, smart, and weird.

Katie locked the door behind us, keeping Squirt out. She hates him.

"Hannah, this is just plain crazy," she began. "You're sitting there, playing chess with my brother, and suddenly a huge bandage appears on your head. What's going on?"

Now, here's the thing. Even Katie, my very best friend, had a hard time believing the angel story when I told her about Australia. So I hadn't told her *everything*. I could only tell her a little bit. Otherwise, she might think I'm going off the deep end and start avoiding me or something. I know friends are supposed to be there for you all the time, and believe everything you tell them, no matter what, but I still wanted to be very careful.

"I'm on another mission," I said, sitting on Kate's bed.

"Don't tell me! You got punched in the head by an angel, right?" she said, all giggly. She put a pillow in her lap and rested her chin on her hands, as if she was all set for a good story.

"Uh, not exactly," I answered. "But during my chess game, right now, I got sent to Kenya."

"Africa?" she chimed back. "You've got to be kidding."

"Yes," I said. "And no on the kidding part."

"But you were here the whole time, Hannah. How can you be in two places at once?"

"I have no idea," I said, shaking my head. "It must be angelic time or something. But I'm in a huge hurry to get back to Africa, and I need your help."

Katie blinked a few times. I know what that means. She wasn't quite sure she believed me.

"Hannah, I'm worried that this angel thing might not be as real as you think," said Katie. She sounded really concerned.

See what I mean? If I don't tell her anything, I push my best friend away. If I tell her too much,

I push her away, too. I don't like the way this angel thing creates trouble between us.

"Can we talk about all the angel stuff when I finish my mission?" I asked. I was worried that Lyra might send me back to Africa at any moment. I had to figure a few things out before I got whisked back there. "*Pleeease,* Katie, please don't ask me to prove anything to you right now, okay? You'll just have to trust me."

"Okay," she said quietly. To prove her loyalty, she gave me our secret hand signal. I'll explain it to you some other time, when somebody's not dying in Kenya.

"I need to go over all my clues so far," I said, opening my journal.

Katie took one of her flying dance-class leaps off the bed. She knelt on the floor and rubbed her head into the carpet. Then she raised herself into an upside-down yoga position. She thinks better that way. Or that's what she says, anyway. Sometimes *I* just have to trust *her*.

"I'm ready," she said. "Shoot."

I told her about Mcheshi and the twenty-two hours I had left to save her life.

Katie's thinking position

"This *is* serious," said Katie, sounding awed.

Then I told her about Sala and Kisululu's

grandmother and the pearl and the medicine man and the chess queen and my dream. I told her I had no idea what the "green" clue meant.

"Tell me what Mcheshi said again," Katie instructed, still standing on her head.

"Well, I'm not absolutely sure," I said. "But I did catch three words: 'Lulu. Green. Leave.' With a few *ohhh*s and *ooo*s and *ahhh*s in between."

"Are you sure she was telling you to leave the hospital?" Katie said.

"What do you mean?" I asked.

"Maybe she was saying *leaf*. You know, as in 'the tree has *green leaves*,'" said Katie.

That hadn't even occurred to me. Lulu could be a green leaf. That seemed to make sense. Maybe it was a healing green leaf that some woman who spoke a different language would know about.

Katie lowered her legs to the floor and rolled back, making her body into a perfect arc. Then she suddenly flipped forward and sprang to her feet.

"We're going downstairs to get on the computer!" she announced.

"NOW?" I said. "But—"

"It's the fastest way to find what we're looking for," she insisted. "Come on, hurry!"

We tore down the stairs with Squirt at our heels and made it to the landing at the same time.

Katie landed quietly. I clattered loudly on the wood floor.

We both looked down at my feet. I still had the sandals on! They were pretty dirty, too.

"Where did you get those?" Katie asked. "They look like something our moms would wear."

I was insulted. Not that we don't like our moms or anything, but we'd never dress in the same stuff they wear, you know?

"I was wearing them in Kenya," I said. "And I don't think they're ugly." Actually I *liked* the way they looked.

"They're pretty dirty, Hannah," said Katie, turning up her nose. "And they smell bad, too."

"Hey, that's probably cow dung!" I said excitedly. "Can you believe it? Cow dung from Kenya, right here on my shoes!"

Katie did not share my new enthusiasm about cow dung. You had to see a house made out of it to appreciate it, I guess.

Anyway, I followed Katie right to the computer, and she got us on the Internet.

"Let's check under 'healing plants,'" said Katie. "Just in case I'm right about the leaf thing."

She pulled up some interesting information, but there was nothing under "lulu."

I checked my watch. THIRTY-NINE HOURS was still flashing. Whew! No time seemed to have passed in Kenya since I'd gotten back to Wisconsin. I was hoping I wouldn't hear Lyra's music quite yet. I wasn't ready to leave.

Katie grabbed my arm. "Hannah, look at this! It's some weird code that's coming out of nowhere!"

There on the screen was a message, gradually appearing symbol by symbol. I recognized the symbols right away. The message was written in Lorielle's code! I started jumping up and down.

"Print it out, Katie!" I shouted. "Quick! Print it out *now!*"

Chapter 13

Simba!

Katie and I stared at the printer in shock as the code printed out. The letters were coming out in shimmery silver!

"This is so weird, Hannah!" Katie said. "We just have regular ink in our printer!"

"It's not weird," I told her. "It's an angel message! Lorielle probably sent it. She writes everything in code!"

I dug into my backpack and pulled out my trusty decoder.

"Hannah! A decoder!" Katie screamed, pinching my arm. She has a nasty habit of pinching me when she gets excited. "That's so cool!"

The decoder was the one angel thing that stayed in my backpack after my trip to Australia.

Everything else had turned back into my regular school stuff: books and papers and pens.

As I carefully translated the message, Katie kept looking from me to the decoder to the message in total amazement. "Amazing! Incredible! Awesome!" she said over and over.

I finished writing the new message into my journal.

Katie screamed again and just about pinched my arm black-and-blue.

"I knew it!" she cried. "Healing green leaves!"

Suddenly it wasn't Katie yelling over my shoulder anymore. It was somebody else.

"Simba!" a voice was calling.

Simba. Well, that was familiar. I saw a movie once where they had a lion named Simba. That's when I realized that Katie was gone and I was back in Kenya, sitting in the same field I'd left from.

Carefully, I got to my feet so I could see over the tall grasses. My worst African nightmare was right in front of me. It took me less than a split second to know what *simba* means in Swahili: "lion!" And there was a *simba* sitting twenty feet away from me.

The lion had huge teeth and a huge mane. There was nothing between the two of us but air and grass.

My view of the lion

"Hatari!" I heard. I could tell that was a warning, like "Stop! Danger!"

I did not budge. I did not breathe. I did not even blink.

The voice belonged to a man who was slowly, *slowly* walking toward me. His face and body were painted, and a mane of wild black feathers surrounded his head. He wore a black cape and had long orange-red hair. To my horror, he was carrying a spear!

I was terrified!

Should I make a run for it, to the *enkang?* No. If you run from a lion, Kisululu had told me, he'll think you're prey. There is no way a human can outrun a lion. If you run, you're lunch meat.

So I just stand there, my journal in one hand and a pen in the other, with a lion twenty feet away and a terrifying guy with a spear, walking very tall, his head held high, moving right toward us.

If you angels want me to finish this trip and save Mcheshi, get me out of here, I pleaded silently. *Get me out of here* NOW.

The man kept approaching. The lion sat very still. My heart was pounding so loud I could hear it drumming in my ears. The man drew closer. My ears drummed louder. The man walked right past the lion, seeming unafraid. Still the lion did not move.

When the man reached the spot where I was

standing, he didn't stop or even turn his head. He glanced at me sideways without a word and kept walking. I knew he wanted me to walk beside him, with the same slow, slow steps. It was the only way out.

Inside, I was cowering. But I held my head high, the way the painted, black-feathered man did, and pretended to be brave.

Soon we were beside the *enkang*, far from the lion. I thought I was going to collapse from fright. My whole body started shaking, and I could hardly catch my breath.

"Thank you, thank you," I told the man.

He nodded. He still looked terrifying in his feathers and his paint. But now I knew he wasn't scary. He had saved my life.

He walked into the *enkang* with me. Kisululu and Sala hurried toward us.

"What happened, Hannah?" they asked, looking from my drained face to the spearman's calm face.

I told them how I'd been so upset about how badly my mission was going that I'd forgotten their warnings about snakes and lions. I'd completely forgotten I wasn't supposed to sit in the grass.

Sala put her arms around me. "You were so lucky, Hannah," she said.

"The man who saved you is a warrior," said

Kisululu, nodding toward my new friend. "He is called a *murran*." (Kisululu pronounced it mur-RAHN.) "In training, warriors are taught how to walk with lions." He gazed at the fierce-looking man with admiration.

"Kisululu may soon train to be a *murran*, too," Sala told me. "Boys train for seven years. Then they practice as warriors for seven more years." I thought it sounded like joining the army for a very long time.

"Do warriors ever get eaten by lions?" I asked.

Kisululu translated for the young warrior. "No," he said, turning back to me, "because they would never walk with a hungry lion or a mother lion with cubs. That would be walking into the jaws of death."

"How did you know that lion wouldn't attack you just now?" I asked the warrior through Kisululu.

"That lion had just finished eating. He was lazy, ready for a nap." Boy, had I lucked out! A lion with a full stomach!

"Also, the *murran* is wearing camphor," Kisululu added. "Lions don't like the smell."

Neither did I. It smelled like Squirt the ferret and the Lamu hospital at the same time.

Then the warrior held something out to me.

"It's a bone from a giraffe," Kisululu told me. He didn't know the bone's name in English. He pointed to my shoulder blade.

"That's the scapular bone," I said. We had just learned that in science, and I felt like a smarty-pants, knowing its correct name. Finally *I* was able to tell someone something they didn't know!

"Why is he showing it to me?" I asked.

"He says he had the bone in his hand as he walked toward you," said Kisululu. "If the lion had attacked you, he would have shoved the bone into the lion's mouth."

The *murran* stretched out his arm, straight as an arrow, holding the bone in his hand. He thrust it forward, as if he were shoving the bone down the throat of a lion. It looked as if his whole hand would end up in the lion's mouth! I shuddered. I've never in my whole life imagined anything so brave.

"You mean, he'd really shove his hand into the lion's mouth like that?" I asked, amazed.

"Yes," said Kisululu. "The bone locks the lion's jaw so he can't bite. Then the *murran* kills the lion with his spear."

"Do you kill a lot of lions?" I asked. I hoped not.

"Never," said the warrior through Kisululu.

"Only to save the life of a person who is attacked."

I thought of the difference between being a boy in Geneva, Wisconsin, and being a boy in the Masai tribe of Kenya. It made me laugh to think that Jimmy Fudge thinks he's so cool and tough! I'd like to see *him* alone in a field with a lion.

No question who'd survive *that* little showdown.

Chapter 14

Giving Up

When the *murran* left, I pulled Sala aside.

"I think I know who Lulu is!" I told her. I had been so excited about the silver message, and now I had exactly twenty-one hours left to wrap up this mission.

"Who?" asked Sala, her eyes wide.

"She, or rather, *it* is a green plant that will heal Mcheshi," I said excitedly.

"Lulu's a plant?" Sala asked. She sounded doubtful.

Sala nodded. "Yes. She uses plants and herbs to heal people. If Lulu is an herb, Grandma Sala will know about it!"

Grandma Sala? Had I heard right?

"Her name is the same as yours?" I asked.

"Yes," Sala said. "It's traditional in her tribe to

name the first granddaughter after the father's mother."

In *her* tribe? This was great!

"So she isn't Masai?" I pressed. "Where was she born?" I held my breath, waiting for her answer.

"Uganda. Why?"

I just about burst by now. I almost pinched Sala the way Katie always pinches me, I was so excited.

"That's it! I have to see her right away!" I cried. "I know she's the one, Sala! She's the mystery woman the *laibon* was talking about!"

Sala looked surprised.

"That is wonderful!" she exclaimed. Then her face suddenly dropped.

"There's one problem," Sala said. "My grandmother has been very ill for a long time. We know she's dying."

"Oh, I'm so sorry," I said. I felt terrible for Sala and her family.

"She might not have the strength to talk with you about the *dawa,*" Sala said. She frowned, looking very disappointed.

I didn't know what to say. How could I ask Sala to talk to her grandmother about me and my problem at a time like this? It seemed pretty rude and unfeeling. But Mcheshi needed me—and Lulu.

"I'm sorry, Sala," I said again. "I just don't

know what to do." I shrugged helplessly.

Sala hesitated.

"I will try to talk with my grandmother," she said. "But she can barely speak."

"Thanks, Sala," I said. "That would be great."

Sala left to go see her grandma. I sat down on a rock and waited. What else could I do? I knew Grandma Sala was the person the angels had told me about. It didn't make sense to go searching anyplace else.

I waited for a long time. I kept thinking that Sala might come out with good news. But Sala didn't come out at all.

The sun went down. The men put the thorny lion branches across the village entrance. The women started making supper, but I wasn't the least bit hungry.

The stars came out, but Sala didn't.

There were so many stars now, they looked like a blanket covering the sky. I thought about the ones on my bedroom ceiling at home. They had seemed so beautiful and magical to me when I couldn't wait for my next angel assignment. Now the stars in Africa reminded me that this was the last night of my mission. My three days were almost up. And I still had no *dawa*.

I dropped my head into my hands, feeling miserable. My watch said 10:10 HOURS. Even if Sala's grandmother *was* the mystery woman—even if she had the green lulu leaves for

Mcheshi—it was too late. I had failed on my mission.

Just then, my thoughts were interrupted by a voice, a whisper. It was saying something in a language I didn't understand.

Another angel message? I wondered with a sigh. Probably from Lorielle, since it needed decoding.

"You're too late, Lorielle," I said out loud. "It's all over. I blew it."

The voice spoke again. This time I recognized it. It wasn't Lorielle's voice. It was Sala's dad. What was he doing here?

Sala and Kisululu's father repeated what he had said.

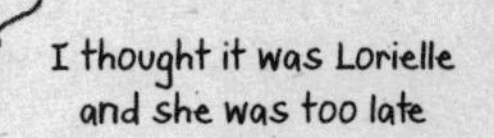
I thought it was Lorielle and she was too late

"Erisyo laikin o kaa. That's Swahili," he said. "It means: 'Defeat and death are the same thing.'"

"What?" I said, confused.

"It's an expression we use in Kenya. And it is quite true."

Defeat. Tears flooded my eyes and trickled down my cheeks. I guess they'd just been all stored up, waiting to finally come out.

"Sorry," I said to Sala and Kisululu's father. I hate crying in front of other people. Especially ones I hardly know.

"Don't be sorry for crying," he said softly. He sat down beside me. "Only be sorry for giving up."

I sniffed a bit and rubbed my eyes. "Even if I found the *dawa*, there's no way I can get back to Lamu in time for Mcheshi."

I showed him my flashing watch. Nine and a half hours.

"You never know what can happen if you keep on trying," he said.

Just then, our voices were drowned out by a loud, buzzing engine. A small white plane was circling over our heads. A few moments later, it landed nearby. On the side of the plane, in big red letters, was written: FLYING DOCTORS' SOCIETY.

Sala's dad immediately jumped up.

"I called the doctors from Nairobi before I left," he said. "Grandma Sala has been getting sicker. They have come to take her to the hospital in the city."

Doctors came flying all the way out here in airplanes! I was impressed.

"Come with me," Sala's dad said.

I followed him to the plane. Two people, a doctor and a pilot, got out. The pilot looked as if he might be a doctor, too. He was carrying a black medicine bag.

"I'm afraid I may have called you too late," Sala's father told them sadly. "My mother is very weak now. She would never make it to a hospital. We believe it is best that she stay here with us."

I couldn't believe Sala and Kisululu's father didn't want the doctors to help. Was he just going to let Grandma Sala die?

"Defeat and death are the same thing," I told him, tugging on his sleeve. "Don't you think the doctors could help?"

Sala and Kisululu's dad looked at me very seriously. "This is different, Hannah. You do not understand. It is my mother's time to die. She knows it. I know it."

I remembered Demi telling me it wasn't Mcheshi's time to die yet. Was it possible it really *was* Grandma Sala's time?

"I'm sorry for your trouble," he told the doctors. "Please come inside for something to eat."

We all went into the *enkang*. As we stepped inside the village, my friends' dad said to me, "Hannah, you must go in and say good-bye to Kisululu and Sala now."

"Good-bye?" I asked in surprise. What did he mean?

"*Dawa* or no *dawa,* it's time you got back to Lamu, Hannah. Your parents must be worried about you."

"But how will I get back?" I asked.

"We'll find a way," Kisululu and Sala's father said.

"We're flying back to the east coast," the pilot

spoke up. "Your daughter is welcome to come along with us."

"Daughter?" I said. "But—"

Sala and Kisululu's father smiled.

"She's been my daughter for three days now," he said, patting me on the head. "Now it's time to send her back to her real parents. We'll take you up on the offer."

I nodded. I knew I might as well leave. I felt as if I had a neon sign hanging around my neck that said THIS GIRL FAILED HER MISSION. In my mind, it was blinking on and off. My mission was truly over now. I knew it, and so did everybody else.

The least I could do was be there with poor Mcheshi.

Chapter 15

The Healing Tree

Just as we reached Grandma Sala's house, Kisululu came running out. He was bursting with news, I could tell.

"Hannah!" he called, hurrying toward me. "Our grandmother wants to see you!"

I couldn't believe my ears. "She *does?*" I said. "Are you sure it's okay?"

"Yes," said Kisululu, tugging on my sleeve. "Come, she's waiting for you."

He led me inside the hut to his grandmother's bed. She was lying on a raised-up area like the one I'd slept on last night, covered with a soft blanket of cowhide.

It was dark inside the hut, except for the fire. It took a few minutes for my eyes to adjust. As soon as they did, I thought I was going to faint! "It's *her!*" I cried, my voice cracking from shock. "The queen!"

Kisululu stood back and stared at me as if I'd lost all my marbles.

"This is Hannah," Sala whispered to her grandma. She frowned at me as if to say, "Please don't embarrass us in front of my grandmother."

But I couldn't calm down. I was bubbling over with excitement. It was absolutely, positively *her*. The chess queen! The Lulu lady!

I fumbled in my pocket for my chess piece. I pulled out the queen. Sala and Kisululu gasped when they saw it.

The chess queen in my pocket

"She has the same face as Grandma!" Sala said to Kisululu, sounding amazed. "The same forehead, the same wrinkles..."

"The same nose, the same smile..." Kisululu continued, peering over Sala's shoulder.

"And most of all, look at those eyes! This is unbelievable!" cried Sala.

This picture took a long time to draw—can you tell?

Grandma Sala

She rushed over to show the chess piece to Grandma Sala. Grandma smiled and gave me a sweet look. Her eyes danced like twinkling stars. I swear, it did seem as if she had totally expected me to come!

"Grandma speaks Lugandan and a little

English," Sala said, handing me back the chess piece. Kisululu was still staring at it in awe. I passed the queen to him, and he held it like a treasure.

"Keep it," I said. "Please." I knew it was important for him to have it. I'd deal with David later.

"Anyway," Sala went on, "I'll translate from Grandma's native language, Lugandan. She has some questions for you, Hannah."

Grandma began to speak. Her voice was very weak. I could barely hear her. Sala had to lean in very close.

"She wants to know what the doctors called Mcheshi's illness," said Sala.

"Malaria," I said.

"And she asks the name of the medicine you're searching for."

"I have no idea," I said with a sigh. "All I know is that I'm looking for some kind of green leaves."

"Aha," said the old woman from her bed. I figured "aha" meant the same in every language. She knew what I was talking about.

"Lulu leaves," I added hopefully.

Grandma Sala said a long word that I didn't quite catch. I thought I heard "lulu" in the middle of it, but I wasn't sure. Then the old woman smiled a sweet, bright smile.

"Why is she smiling?" I whispered to Sala.

"She says that Lulu is right outside, waiting for you," said Sala. She turned and said something to Kisululu.

Kisululu slapped his forehead. "Of course!" he said. "Why didn't *we* figure that out?"

Kisululu and Sala cracking up

I was standing there, wishing they would all let me in on what they were talking about.

"OH-MOO-*LULU*-ZA!" Sala said to me, as if I would understand.

I threw up my hands in bewilderment.

"OH-MOO-*LULU*-ZA!" Kisululu repeated, looking right at me.

This time I really listened to the word. It sounded exactly like what Mcheshi had been saying. A bunch of *ohh*s and *ooo*s and *ahhh*s, with *lulu* in the middle!

Grandma Sala reached for my hand and held it gently for a moment. I think she was gathering her strength to talk. She whispered something to Sala.

Sala immediately scooted over to the corner and picked up a basket.

"Follow me," she said.

We hurried outside into the garden. It was all wild and weedy. The moonlight glowed on fuzzy plants, tiny bunches of flowers, and gigantic bushes. They were completely different from the maples and marigolds we have at home.

"This is Grandma Sala's pharmacy," Sala said. "She grows all her herbs for healing out here."

Sala went over to a huge hairy plant, almost the size of a tree. It had pale white flowers that smelled like exotic perfume.

"Hannah, meet Omululuza," Sala said, gesturing as if she was introducing me to an important person.

"No!" I shrieked. "That's the green lulu plant?"

"Omululuza, meet Hannah," Sala went on, teasing. "Hannah's been searching all over Kenya for you."

"I can't believe it!" I cried. I gave that bush one big hug. "So this is what Mcheshi was asking for!"

"Yes," said Sala. "This plant can help cure malaria. It helps take the fever down."

"Fantastic!" I said. "But exactly which part is the *dawa*?" I didn't know if you were supposed to eat the flowers or drink the sap from the trunk or what.

"To get the *dawa* made on time, we're going to have to rush. It's not that easy. First we have to gather leaves," Sala instructed.

Both of us quickly began pulling long gray-green leaves off the plant, one by one. We tossed them into the basket.

"Why didn't you tell me about this plant earlier?" I asked.

"Until Grandma said the whole word, I didn't understand," said Sala. "And I didn't know that Mcheshi would be from Uganda."

"But isn't this called Omululuza in Swahili, too?" I really liked saying it. OH-MOO-*LULU*-ZA. It was a really cool word. I wanted to make a song out of it.

"No," said Sala. "In Kenya, we call this plant something different."

We filled the basket to the brim. Then we rushed inside with our leaves. But when we reached Grandma Sala's bedside, breathless, we stopped in our tracks.

Chapter 16

"Kwa heri, Rafiki"

Sala and I stood there next to Kisululu, staring at Grandma Sala.

She was lying motionless with her eyes closed.

"She's asleep," said Kisululu.

Just then, Grandma Sala's eyelids flickered. She was still alive, thank goodness! I let out a huge sigh of relief.

It took a minute before the frail old woman could speak. Talking seemed to be a struggle, just as it had been for Mcheshi.

"Ten leaves," Grandma muttered. She was speaking English so I could understand. I quickly grabbed my journal from my knapsack and pulled out a pen. I had to get the directions down in case Mcheshi needed more *dawa* later.

Sala took ten leaves from the basket.

"Boiling water," Grandma said. "Cold."

"She means water that we've boiled to kill any germs," Sala explained to me.

Kisululu hurried across the room to a table and got the water.

The old woman began to fade out again. I looked at my watch. Seven hours and fifteen minutes left! How was I ever going to pull this off?

I wanted to say, "Come on, hurry. *Faster*." But I knew we were already moving as fast as we could.

A few more Masai people came in to see Grandma, including Kisululu and Sala's dad. He put his arm around my shoulders.

"All right, my three-day daughter," he said. "The doctors are ready to go whenever you are." I checked my watch again. Seven hours, ten minutes.

"Great!" I said. "As soon as we finish making the *dawa,* I'll be ready." Then I added, "Thanks, my three-day dad." He smiled. Then he went to sit beside his mother, holding her hand.

She struggled to explain to us how to squeeze the leaves, crush them into the water, and filter them. As Sala and Kisululu sped through the work, I took more notes. My writing was really messy because it was all going so fast. Sala and Kisululu moved in a blur, squeezing and crushing leaves to make a deep green liquid that looked like some thick, exotic tea.

But I couldn't help noticing that while we were speeding up, Grandma Sala was slowing down. Her breathing slowed, her words slowed. All the people gathering around her moved very, very slowly, too.

"What's next?" Sala asked her in a hushed voice.

Grandma whispered, "Two spoons." Then after a few long moments, she added, "Three times."

"That means you should give Mcheshi two tablespoons, three times a day," Sala instructed me.

When the remedy was finally ready, Sala gave her grandmother a tiny taste from the jar. The old women smiled and whispered something to her.

"Grandma Sala says it's perfect," Sala said, handing me the jar. I could see tears in her eyes. "It is her last healing. She says she is pleased to help a child live when she is about to die."

I was afraid I was about to burst out crying. But I had to be brave like Grandma Sala and her whole family. I bit my lip.

Sala and Kisululu's dad was gently stroking the old woman's hand. Now everything in the room had grown so slow that it finally all seemed to stop. In the far, far distance, I heard the sound of ancient music, low and deep, with faint drumming. Lyra was on her way! But somehow I knew she wasn't coming to help me. She was coming to be with Grandma Sala.

Just then, I saw something I will never forget in my whole life. The room began to fill with an amazing, starry glow. It was as if the light from every star in the sky had come together at once. And then I saw my angels, all four of them, surrounding Grandma Sala. I swear I could actually *see* them. They were right there, right in that room. And they were just as beautiful as I had imagined them.

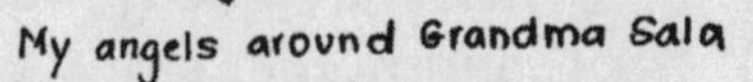

My angels around Grandma Sala

Now I knew—I was absolutely certain—that my angels were real. I hadn't just imagined them. They were so bright, they were almost blinding. I could feel them saying, *Everything is all right.* Grandma Sala would pass into her next life because it was her time. Mcheshi would keep living because it *wasn't* her time. I knew now, from the very bottom of my heart, that this was true.

Gradually, the starry glow began to grow softer. Grandma Sala had died. It was time for her family to be alone together. And it was time for me to go.

I checked my watch. Ten and a half hours. I grasped the *dawa* jar tightly in my hand, as if it were a jar of precious jewels. Then I motioned to the pilot and tiptoed out the doorway of the house.

Kisululu followed me. He walked me to the village gate and pulled back the thorn branches.

"It's very dark," he told me, putting a few pebbles into my hand. "The lions..."

"Don't worry, Kisululu," I assured him. "I won't go walking in the grass. I'm getting right on the plane."

pebbles for the lions

He nodded, smiling.

"Kwa heri, rafiki" he said. "Good-bye, friend."

I gave Kisululu a warm hug. Then I watched him turn around, pull the lion branches back over the entrance, and walk away.

Someday, I hoped, we might see each other again. But now I had to go.

I had a life to save.

Chapter 17

Cloudy, with a Chance of Angels

The airplane's engines roared to life, blowing up a cloud of dust in the night air. The Flying Doctors were ready to go. The pilot helped me on board. It was a tiny plane, with just enough room in the back for someone to lie down on a stretcher.

Suddenly Sala came running toward the plane, waving.

"Good-bye, Hannah!" she shouted. I could hardly hear her over the noise and wind.

I reached my hand out the plane door to give her a farewell shake. She put something in my palm.

Sala handing me a present

"I made it myself!" she yelled. "It's for you so you will always remember me, Hannah!"

"I won't forget you, Sala!" I cried. "How could I ever forget you?"

The pilot shut the door. The doctors couldn't wait for a long good-bye. Neither could I. I belted myself in, and we took off. My watch said 6:10 HOURS.

I looked at Sala's present. It was a beautiful beaded bracelet, blue and red and green. I hooked it on my wrist and twisted the beads around for a long time. I couldn't believe Sala had put every one of them on by hand.

It was all noisy and buzzy in the little plane. I began to feel kind of jittery and woozy. I tried to think about other things to take my mind off my queasy stomach.

I picked up a pamphlet from the side pocket of my seat. It was all about the Flying Doctors' Society. The flier said these doctors travel all over Kenya, saving lives. They fly to wherever there's an emergency. What a job!

If I got to Mcheshi in time, maybe I could become an honorary Flying Doctor. Thinking about that kept my mind occupied for a while. I thought about getting Flying Doctor wings pinned on me, in front of a crowd. I thought about how maybe I really could be a doctor when I got older. I thought about anything I could to forget about the time ticking, ticking away.

It didn't work. I still checked my watch just about every minute. We were zooming along just fine. Then a horrendous thing happened. A major fog rolled in.

All I could see out the window of the plane was a thick, cloudy white fog. I started to get an itchy, sweaty, panicky feeling. Our plane was bumping around like a little lost toy trying to find its way home.

"We might have to make an emergency landing," the pilot yelled back to the doctor.

"No!" I shouted. "We can't do that!" (As if I had a say in their decision.) But I knew if we landed the plane, all hope for Mcheshi was lost.

"Please," I begged my angels. "Do something! Please help the pilot get us through this fog."

The plane continued to bounce through the foggy clouds. I felt queasier and queasier.

"It's not getting any better," the pilot hollered.

"Maybe we'd better land and wait it out," the doctor yelled back.

I squeezed my eyes shut.

"Can you make a star path, Aurora?" I asked. "Please! We have to get there!"

All of a sudden, the plane picked up speed

and blasted forward. I swear I could see stars being tossed out ahead, clearing the fog. We shot through the sky like a rocket. I held on tightly to the armrest with one hand and clung to my *dawa* jar with the other. My head was forced back against the seat from the incredible speed. I imagined an angel on each side of the plane, an angel in back, and Aurora leading the way.

I don't know if the doctors saw any angels, but I can tell you one thing for sure—the pilot flew that plane like an arrow speeding straight to its mark. At exactly two hours, ten minutes, we came out of that fog. Through the window, I could see the sun rising over Lamu Island. We touched down on the mainland, right near the ferry-boat dock.

"Thank you!" I shouted to the Flying Doctors as I jumped off the plane. The pilot looked a little shaken, as if he didn't know what had hit him. If I'd told him what I thought had happened, he would have been even more shaken up. He probably wouldn't have believed me anyway.

"Will you make it on time?" the doctor called after me.

"I'm sure going to try!" I called back, and raced toward the dock, the *dawa* jar in hand.

I *had* to make it!

Chapter 18

Wings on My Feet

I ran for the ferry, still clutching the precious jar of *dawa*. I reached the boat just before it sailed. Luckily, I still had enough shillings left for the fare. It was pure torture, riding the slow ferry across to Lamu. I wanted the angels to speed it up like the plane and get to the other side instantly. But this time, nothing happened.

dawa for Mcheshi

My watch was ticking down. 1:20 HOURS… 1:15 HOURS…1:10 HOURS.

I was almost ready to dive off the boat and swim. Of course, I'd never make it across to the island. This was the Indian Ocean, after all. I'm not that great a swimmer, and besides, there were probably sharks in the water or something.

When we finally got to the dock, I took a flying leap off the boat. From that point on, I felt as if

I was running an Olympic race. I even ripped off my sandals because I figured I could run faster in my bare feet.

I tore through the narrow, winding streets, careering past black-veiled women. I raced under old archways, past donkeys, and through a bunch of goats eating their breakfast out of the garbage.

For some reason, I seemed to know exactly where I was going. The angels must have been guiding me again. Luckily, there was no wind, so the coconuts stayed safely on the trees.

When I finally saw the hospital in front of me, my watch was flashing 0:30 HOURS.

I raced through the front door, tore down a corridor, and crashed right into Mr. Ali, the nurse. What perfect luck! (Or was it luck?)

"Whoa!" he said. He probably recognized me by my bandage.

"Is Mcheshi okay?" I said breathlessly, tearing down the hall. I had no time to stop, not even for Mr. Ali. He was right behind me.

"She's very sick," he said. "We found her parents."

I dashed across the finish line, which was the doorway to Mcheshi's room, and rushed toward the little girl's bed. She looked worse than ever. Her face was flushed and she was barely moving at all. Her parents were sitting by her side, each holding one of her hands.

"I have a *dawa* for Mcheshi!" I burst out.

The parents looked shocked. I don't think they knew what to do. I guess it must have been pretty strange to have me barge in like that.

"Who is this?" the mom asked the dad in English. "And what is *dawa?*"

"Medicine," the dad answered.

The father spoke Swahili. So I guess it was Mcheshi's mother who was Ugandan.

I thrust the jar in front of them and pulled out the stopper. I pointed inside.

"Oh-moo-*lulu*-za," I said. I had no time to explain. We had to get some of the remedy into Mcheshi's frail body right away. "It's a Lugandan word for..."

But the mother cut me off.

"Omululuza!" she cried, her face lighting up. "I know exactly what it is!"

She took the jar and held it just the way I had, as if it was a precious treasure. She put a dab of the remedy on her tongue and passed the jar to her husband, who tasted it, too.

"Yes!" they both said. "Thank you!"

I thought Mcheshi's mom would smother me, she hugged me so tight! Then she turned to Mr. Ali, who was standing in the doorway.

"My daughter needs this medicine. Can you give it to her?" she asked.

"I'm sorry," he said. "Because of hospital rules—I can't administer homemade remedies."

My heart sank.

"But *you* can certainly give it to her," he went on.

My heart rose back up where it belonged. *Phew!*

Mcheshi's mother fed her daughter a spoonful of the *dawa,* a little bit at a time.

"Mcheshi will be better in a few days now, I am sure of it!" the mother assured me, tears streaming down her cheeks. "How can we ever thank you? What can we do?"

"Please just give Mcheshi my address," I said. "I'd love to be her pen pal!"

I scribbled my name and address on a page of my journal, ripped it out, and gave it to them.

Mcheshi's parents began to tell me the whole story of how their daughter had become ill and wandered away from the aunt she'd been visiting.

"She wandered onto the ferry by mistake," said the mother.

"We had no idea where she disappeared to," said the dad, "until her aunt saw a drawing posted on a tree. It had been apparently made by some children."

"It was a picture of an angel," said the mother. "And Mcheshi's name was written below it. The sign said CAN YOU FIND HER PARENTS?"

I stayed there with Mcheshi and her parents for a few minutes. Then, suddenly,

Whew! I did it!

my watch began flashing 0:00 HOURS. At the same time, I heard that distant drumming sound once again, joined by Lyra's sweet, misty music. Before I could even say good-bye to Mcheshi and her parents, my time was up.

And my mission had been an amazing success!

Chapter 19

It's Your Move!

I was back home in Wisconsin in the blink of an eye. Katie and I were sitting at the computer, staring at a blank screen and a blank print-out.

"Hey! What happened to our silver message?" she wailed. "It was so awesome, and now it's gone!"

"I guess we don't need it anymore," I said.

Katie turned to me and gave a heavy sigh. Then Sala's bracelet suddenly caught her eye.

"Hannah!" she practically screamed. "You're back from a mission again! You didn't go to Africa and come back again while I was sitting here the whole time, did you?"

"I guess I did," I said.

I had to admit, it was good to be back.

"What a great bracelet!" Katie said. I knew she'd want to try it on.

Sala's bracelet

"Can I try it on?" she asked. (See? I can read her mind.)

"Tell me everything," she said, all excited. "Was it a healing green plant? Is Mcheshi okay? Who was the mystery woman?"

Just then, David walked in.

"Later," Katie whispered to me quickly. I nodded. Katie went back to her cello.

"So, are you going to reveal your big secret, Hannah?" he asked. "You can tell me. I'm your favorite next-door neighbor's brother. And I'm extremely trustworthy."

"What are you talking about?" I asked, trying to sound innocent.

"The bandage. That bracelet," he said. "Do you think I'm blind?"

What could I say? This was the second time David had seen me come back with treasures from an angel mission.

"And, uh, by the way—where's the queen from my chess set?" he asked.

"I guess your queen got tired of putting up with that lazy king, and so she took a little trip," I said. "I'll replace her."

I knew I had to change the subject—fast. If I was having a hard time getting Katie to believe my angel stores, David would be absolutely impossible.

"How about if we play a new game? One you've never played before?" I asked David.

I opened my backpack. Sure enough, there was a mancala board inside with a bag of pebbles. I showed them to David.

"What do you think?" I asked.

David eyed the board suspiciously.

"Okay, on one condition," he said finally. "You can't make up your own rules as you go along."

"I *never* do that!" I objected. David was right, of course. I *do* like to change the rules occasionally if it makes the game more interesting.

I spilled the pebbles out onto the rug. They weren't Kenyan pebbles. They were made of glass, in gem colors—they looked like rubies and emeralds and sapphires. They reminded me of Africa—the spices and silks, the Indian Ocean. And—how could I forget?—my very own island.

"Where did you get this game, anyway?" David asked.

"From Zanzibar," I said dramatically. "You know, the place where pirates used to find all those precious jewels!"

He rolled his eyes. "Yeah, right!"

I told him the rules of mancala, all of them.

"It's your move," I said.

It would probably take David a while to get into this new game, since he's a major perfectionist. He wouldn't want to make a wrong move.

Me & David playing mancala

I picked up a yellow mancala pebble and twirled it in front of my eye. The light from the window shone through it, shimmering all golden, like the sun. I wonder what kind of treasures lay ahead, on my next mission for the angels?

"Your move!" said David, interrupting my thoughts.

"Hold on a minute," I said.

I was having a hard time tearing my eye away from that pebble. For a split second, flying through that golden sun, I believed I saw an angel.

Kwa heri, rafiki! (Good-bye, friend!)

COOL KENYAN STUFF

Coconuts—When they're growing on palm trees, you see the husk, which is green or tan (and *really* big!). You open them up to find the brown seed (what we buy at the grocery store), which has coconut milk inside. In windy weather, as I found out, coconuts fall from the trees.

Elephant—You can tell the difference between an African elephant and an Indian elephant by its ears. African elephants have ears shaped like Africa. Indian elephants have ears shaped like India. (Cool, huh?) Also, African elephants are bigger. They weigh 12,000 pounds and are 13 feet tall. Here's another amazing elephant fact I learned from Sala: You know that elephants trumpet, snort, and roar, but did you know they sometimes *snore?* True!

Enkang—A village where the Masai people live. The homes inside, which the women build, are made of cow dung. At night, the men cover the entrance to the *enkang* with thick, thorny branches to keep out the lions and hyenas.

Flying Doctors' Society—Group of doctors who fly small planes into remote parts of Kenya for medical emergencies. They usually take the injured or sick person in their plane to a hospital in Nairobi for treatment.

Hair—Long hair is a sign of power to the Masai. Men grow their hair long, and the warriors dye their hair with red ocher. Women usually shave their heads or have short hair. It's hard to tell the men from the women at first. But after a while, you get used to it.

Herbs—Sometimes at home we use herbs for healing colds (Grandma Zoe gives me chamomile or echinacea tea when I'm sick). But in Kenya, there are many herbal doctors, and they have whole gardens full of plants that are used to heal colds, fever, malaria, and other illnesses. If the herbs don't work, people usually go to the hospital for treatment.

Indian Ocean—It's my favorite of all the oceans because it sounds so faraway and mysterious. I love the names of its arms, too: the Bay of Bengal, the Red Sea, the Arabian Sea. (Aren't they mysterious-sounding?) It's a good thing I didn't dive off the ferry to swim because the Indian Ocean is full of sharks, barracudas, and sailfish.

Jewelry—Masai men and women wear beautiful colorful beaded necklaces, earrings, and headbands. Long earlobes are a sign of beauty, so the

Masai pierce their ears and put wooden plugs into the holes until the holes get very big. When Masai women get married, they wear long beaded earrings in their long earlobes. Masai men spend more time working on being beautiful than women do.

Kenyan shillings—The currency (money) used in Kenya. There are about sixty Kenyan shillings to an American dollar.

Lamu Island—A tropical island in the Indian Ocean that used to be a trading center for spices, silks, and perfumes from Zanzibar. (Exotic, huh?) It's like the *Arabian Nights* there, with old streets and women in black veils (called *yashmaks*) and secret carved doorways everywhere. To get around the island, you ride a donkey.

Mancala—A game played with pebbles and a wooden board. Years ago, men played serious mancala games in order to win women. The winner got a wife as the prize! Now mancala is played just for fun all over Africa. Sometimes it's called *bao*.

Masai—A tribe of people who live mostly in western Kenya, on the Masai Mara plains. For centuries, they were nomads, traveling wherever there was food for themselves and their cattle. Now laws prohibit them from killing wild animals for food, so most people have settled in villages. The Masai love children and baby animals. Sometimes they bring young animals into their houses to sleep at night, which I think is so cool.

Medicine man—The Masai call their medicine man a *laibon*. He is always an elder and the healer in the village. Sometimes he does the healing himself, and sometimes he helps people find what they need to cure their illnesses.

Mount Kilimanjaro—The highest mountain in Africa, over 19,000 feet high. I also saw Mount Kenya on my trip—it's about 17,000 feet, the second-highest peak. Both of these mountains are extinct volcanoes. That means they used to erupt, but now they don't.

Murran—A Masai warrior. When a boy turns fifteen, he becomes a junior warrior for seven years, then a senior warrior for seven more years. Each warrior carries a knife, a stick, and a spear. His job is to find food and water for the cattle. A young warrior in training wears black, including a black feathered headdress. Later he dresses in a red cloak, like the senior warriors.

Nairobi—The capital of Kenya, Nairobi is a very modern and busy city.

Names—Until a Masai child is five months old, he or she has only a nickname. Babies get their real names in a sacred ceremony, when an elder chooses a name that especially fits that child. The elder tells the child to live long, be brave, respect the poor, and become as famous as Mount Kilimanjaro.

Omululuza—An evergreen that grows 4 to 10 feet high. It looks like a tree because it's so big, but it's really a shrub. It is very powerful in reducing fever and treating malaria. It is found in the courtyard of every herbal doctor in Uganda, and many people there use it for healing. Its scientific name is *Vernonia amygdalina.* (Omululuza, the Lugandan name, is much more fun to say, don't you think?) The omululuza shrub also grows in Kenya, by the way.

Swahili—The language spoken in Kenya. It is really called "Kiswahili," but in English we just call it "Swahili." Many Kenyans also speak English, which was lucky for me. Besides Swahili, there are over 1,000 dialects spoken in Africa. (Amazing!) Maa, the language of the Masai people, is one of them.

Transportation—The train I took from Mombasa to Nairobi is famous. When it was built in 1899, it was called "The Lunatic Express" because it was the first train to travel through parts of Africa that seemed secret and dangerous to the British. Its route is 667 miles long and ends in Uganda. The train gets stopped pretty often by elephants, giraffes, zebras, and other wild animals. (The animals, of course, have the right of way!)

A LITTLE DICTIONARY FROM MY TRIP

Swahili Words

Dawa	DAH wah	Medicine
Hatari	ha TAR ee	Danger
Jambo	JAHM bo	Hello
Kwa heri	kwah HARRY	Good-bye
Lulu	LOO loo	Pearl
Rafiki	rah FEE kee	Friend
Safari	*(You know this one!)*	Journey
Simba	SIM bah	Lion
Ugali	oo GOLLY	Paste made of cornmeal and water

Maa Words

Enkang	EN kahng	Masai village
Laibon	LY bahn	Medicine man
Murran	Mur RAHN	Warrior

Some African Names

Kisululu	KEY SOO LOO LOO	A Masai boy's name
Mcheshi	Muh CHESH EE	Swahili (It means *playful*)
Mzee	Muh ZAY	Swahili (A way to say "Sir")
Sala	SOLL AH	Lugandan (It means *Sarah* in English)

A lot of names start with M in Swahili. The M's are tricky because they have consonants after them. The people draw them out as if they're humming "mmm," but you can say a short "muh" sound and the people still understand you.

Here's a sneak peek at

Hannah and the Angels #3:
Mexican Treasure Hunt

Available starting Fall 1998 wherever books are sold!

When I caught the falling orange, it was warm, as if it had been sitting in the sun. Something wasn't right. I glanced down at the fruit. The oranges were still stacked in front of me, but there were no more apples. Avocados were piled beside the oranges now, but there were no blueberries in sight. I looked to the right and saw tons of peppers—red, yellow, orange, green. And beside the peppers were...

I froze in fear. I didn't even want to think about what I'd just seen.

"Mom?" I called weakly.

I didn't get an answer. I should have known. My mom was gone. And I wasn't in the grocery store anymore. I was somewhere else, and I don't think I wanted to be there.

Slowly, I turned my eyes back, past the red peppers, past the green ones. And there they were again! Skulls! And bones! Whole skeletons!

I backed away, right into a lady with a chicken. Chicken feathers flew all over the place, like snow.

Suddenly everything turned into chaos. Oranges were rolling, chicken feathers were snowing, and I was screaming.

And at my feet were a bunch of tiny rolling skulls, their black eye sockets staring up at me…

Earn Your Golden Wings!

If you've acted like Hannah and helped someone, you are eligible to receive a special *Hannah and the Angels* golden wings gift. Fill out the coupon below with details of how you acted like an angel (attach additional sheets if necessary).

To receive your FREE gift, mail to:

Random House Children's Publishing
Earn Your Wings Promotion
201 East 50th Street, MD 30-2
New York, NY 10022

Name: KATIE ROY Age: 8

Address: 411 Head St. N. Strathroy Ont. N7G-2K1

I was an angel when I yelled help when Madi my sister spilt hot coffee all over her. And I was only 2 yrs old then.

Available while supplies last. Offer ends March 31, 1999. *All coupons must be received by Random House before 5:00 p.m. EST on that date.* Limit: One per customer. Not valid with other offers. Multiple requests, mechanical reproductions, and facsimiles will not be honored. Reproduction, sale, or purchase of this coupon is prohibited. Random House reserves the right to reject any forms not deemed genuine. Valid only in the United States. Please allow 6-8 weeks for delivery.